LYCAN AND THE PRINCESS

LYCAN CLAIMED
BOOK 1

MILANA JACKS

Lycan and the Princess © Milana Jacks

All rights reserved.

No part of this book may be reproduced in any form or by any electronic or mechanical means, including information storage and retrieval systems, without written permission from the author, except for the use of brief quotations in a book review.

This is a work of fiction. Names, characters, businesses, places, events and incidents are either the products of the author's imagination or used in a fictitious manner. Any resemblance to actual persons, living or dead, or actual events is purely coincidental.

Cover Design by Trif Book Design

1

LENOX

I was born of a traitor and a whore.

Such a birth means I fought for everything I wanted in life. Why should my mating be any different, aye?

First, instead of a lycan female, my mate is of Stenan origin, specifically a former Kilseleian princess who's never worn an apron or picked up a ladle out of a barrel-sized pot to taste the soup she made for supper. While I'm certain that growing up as the princess taught her how to order people around, I doubt she would know how to run a lycan clan alongside me.

The worst thing about my mating?

The princess is eighteen.

Eighteen. I snatch a bottle, pour, and empty the glass down my throat. It's the nastiest bourbon I've ever tasted. In spite of that, I continue drinking it.

I can't remember being eighteen. It feels like a century ago. Almost was a century ago, since I'm closing in on one hundred and one turns this fall. I might look thirty, but as a lycan, I have another hundred turns before any aging shows.

"How old were you when you first shagged?" I ask Rohan, the pirate cousin who brought me to the fairy shores where the king of the Summer Court hid my mate on one of his estates.

"Can't remember." Rohan ponders and presses his lips to a fairy female's ear. He whispers something about her tits. This is one of those times when I curse my excellent hearing.

"Why do you ask?" he says while the female gets up from his lap. He slaps her bottom before she sashays away.

Another fairy comes to stand between his legs. She looks exactly like the one that just left. Twins.

"No reason," I say, watching the other twin return. Now there are two.

"I've known ye forever, mate," Rohan says. "Ye don't yap for no reason." From his pocket, he pulls out a single key and hands it to one lass. They each kiss him on either cheek and leave the upper deck.

"I'm thinking of someone," I say.

More fairies will come soon. They're like flies to honey. It's Summer-fae mating season, and the fae females love the lycan knob. We swell at the base like their fae males, but we're built bigger and smell of forest and rain instead of sea, orchids, and other flowery things I can't name.

"Princess Gloriana, is it?" Rohan asks, a smirk tugging his lips.

I nod. Tall, with long legs and a lean build, I could pin my mate against the wall and not have to bend to enter. She's young and looking for the party, which is why she'll show up tonight instead of staying at home in her estate farther from the court.

Rohan's light blue eyes regard me as I swig from the bottle of dirty bourbon he received from the savages. It goes down rough, much rougher than ale from lycan lands.

I miss the ale. The sooner I can locate the princess, the sooner I can leave the fae court. I'm all sorts of moody over my mate staying in a foreign court. A fae one at that.

Which is why the Summer king promised to deliver her to me. His sister, Fleur, is out with Gloriana tonight, and there's a chance the ladies will attend Rohan's party that's happening below.

I slick back my hair, tuck the slipping strands behind my ears, and wonder what my mate will say when she sees me.

We met only once before, and it was in the aftermath of a horde battle that overthrew her father, who was king at the time. Clearly distressed, Gloriana was skittish and scared when I told her she was mine and that I would protect her. I promised her the loyalty of my clan and my lands, but did not claim her at the time. The next thing I knew, the princess had vanished.

I searched for her everywhere.

I killed a savage male, thinking he'd taken her, and if the savages ever find out I did their male in, they'll plunder the clan lands. All for nothing, since the Summer king took my lass.

Or rather, she went to him and asked him to save her.

Save her. What a sack of shite.

A group of females climbs onto the top deck, and the pixie band perched at the bar turns up the tune. They play something livelier. As if my blood needs more enlivening around the fairies in mating season. My balls are so heavy with seed, I'm surprised they haven't detached and splattered onto the deck.

I grab them and move them around, unsticking them from each other during the summer night's heat.

Five beautiful, scantily dressed fairies of various shapes and sizes start swaying their hips. They smell like the sea and the light oils of the flowers found growing near their shores. Overall, they carry the scents I identify with Summer fairies and not Kilseleians with round ears.

So when I sniff out a Kilseleian female, my heart starts thudding in my ears. I know the scent of my mate. She came here with the group of fae.

She came to the pirate ship seeking the lycan knob, like the other females here tonight.

"She's here," I announce to Rohan, jerking my head toward the group that's eyeballing us like we're candy.

"It's just fairies," he says.

The group of females appears to be all fairies, but the gentle breeze cooling my balls under my kilt also blows the scent of my mate toward me, so I'm sure they're not all fae. Gloriana smells like orange blossom doused in rain. Strong and sexy, and impossible for me not to recognize.

I growl low in my throat. "She's definitely here."

"All right. The Summer king must be disguising her with a glamour. Remember what we talked about."

"I remember."

"I'll remind you anyway. I intend to do business with the Summer king, so we don't want to piss him off. My sources tell me the Kilseleian princess is his pet, so tread with caution."

"She's not his pet."

"You know what I mean by that."

Yeah, I knew, but I hated his choice of words. The Summer king is sheltering Gloriana and providing for her, something I should've done in his place.

Had she fucking let me.

She hid instead.

Well, not for long now.

The scent of orange blossoms grows stronger, and with it, I grow harder, a growl from my chest now a soothing rumble meant to attract a female.

Another fae ascends the steps and joins the group. It's Fleur, the Summer princess, her body sculpted by a divine hand. She exudes beauty and power in her tiny royal dress.

If one can even call it a dress. It covers the female parts and nothing more.

From across the deck, Fleur smiles at me and laces hands with a friend on her right.

"That's the Summer princess," Rohan moans.

"Try not to squirt on her toes."

Rohan snorts. "Won't be easy, but I'll try."

I know what he means. Beautiful fairies in their heat call for a mating.

Fleur tugs her friend toward us, and they walk in our direction hand in hand. Their long, legs capture my attention and hold it until they reach us. The brunette has straight shoulder-length hair and hazel eyes and wears a two-piece outfit. The top wraps around the lass's ample breasts and the bottom wraps around her arse. It's royal blue because that's the color of the season.

Both females approach barefoot, wearing stacks of anklets that will jingle as they're shagged.

Fleur kicks my shin. "Make room on your lap."

I widen my legs, hitting Rohan with my left knee. If I go any wider, my balls will tear off. I love my balls. They'll supply the first heirs of my clan.

Fleur sits on my left thigh. I stiffen. Didn't think she'd sit down. Fucking fairies.

The other female sits on my right thigh. The scent of my mate stuffs my nose, and I adjust my groin before attempting to speak. I open my mouth, but the fae princess presses a finger over my lips.

Blue eyes, a similar color to mine, crinkle at the corners as Fleur says, "It's best if you stay quiet, wolf. You'll ruin the fun with all the mating business."

"Aye, lass. The mating business." I grip Gloriana's hip and squeeze.

My mate giggles as if she likes it, even leans into me, propping an elbow on my shoulder.

Fleur strokes Gloriana's hair. "You have no idea who this lycan is, do you?"

My mate shakes her head and snatches the drink from my hand. She takes a swig and swallows as if the bourbon goes down like water. It does not.

The drink is cheap and nasty.

And the princess should balk at it.

"Nope," Gloriana says, slightly slurring the word, "but he's really hard." She gropes my thigh, her hand squeezing my flesh right near my crotch. If she weren't mine, I'd push her off my lap. But she is mine, and I'm caught off guard.

This is not how I imagined our meeting would go. Not even close.

"What have you done to her?" I bite out.

Fleur stands and stretches her arms high above her head, drawing attention to the scant clothes that lift over her breasts, revealing the curves of the underside. I look away before I start groping my mate.

"I expect her at brunch tomorrow, so be sure she can walk." Fleur winks and leaves us.

Rohan follows the princess.

I snort, surprised he's not crawling after her, tongue out and dragging on the floor.

In a matter of moments, the upper deck clears out, and

my mate and I are alone. The lights dim, and the pixies play something sultry, no doubt music that invites hands to wander.

The female in my lap presses her lips against my cheek.

If I look at her, I can't see through the glamour masking Gloriana's face, so I stare ahead, relying on my scent, something nobody can fool.

"I met a lycan once," she says, her voice sounding ten times more seductive to me than the entire orchestra.

"Yeah?" I squeeze her hip. That lycan better be me. "Tell me about it."

She flips her dark brown hair over her shoulder, but it returns to fall over the side of her face. I'm trying to see through the glamour, but I can't, and I have no idea how long Fleur will keep up this charade. I know this is my mate, and I want to see her face, not the face of this beautiful stranger.

I tuck the soft strands behind her ear.

"Thank you," she says, and locks her pretty eyes with mine. Gloriana's eyes stayed the same color despite the glamour. Hazel, the most common color of eyes for a Stenan female from the tribal lands. Expressive and warm.

"The lycan I met..." Her face moves toward me until our noses are almost touching. I smell bourbon on her breath, along with citrus blossom and feminine arousal that calls to me more than any siren surrounding the boat and singing to the pixie tune.

"He had blue eyes like you."

"Most lycans are blue-eyed."

She nods. "He also had a beard and lots of jewelry." She picks up the hem of my kilt. "And a kilt like this one, but red, not green."

"What was his name?" I ask.

She frowns and chews her lip. The movement makes me leak semen under the kilt. I might come on Rohan's deck.

"You know, I don't recall that he gave me his name."

"Lenox?" I ask.

Her eyes widen as recognition hits her, but still, it's almost as if she remembers me, but not quite. Either it's the booze, or the fairies messed with her somehow. I'll find out later. Right now, she's with me, and I'm going to play along. I've waited a lifetime to hold my mate, and I'm keeping her forever this time around.

Too bad she doesn't know that yet.

"Lenox sounds right." She traces a finger down my jaw. "You're better looking than him."

I shaved my beard, and she likes it better. I'll be shaving for the rest of my life.

"Oh yeah?" I run my nose down her cheek, jaw, and neck, where I inhale loudly. Oh yes, definitely mine. I want to bite her already, mark her slender neck.

A growl rips from my chest.

On my lap, she stiffens, and I take her hand and put it over my torso. I switch from growling to rumbling. I don't purr like a feline, though the rumbling, if done well, sounds as seductive as a feline purr.

My mate leans in closer and runs her hand through my hair.

Mmhm. *Pet me, baby. Pet yer wolf.*

From the corner of my eye, I see her doing something with the left hand that used to rest on my shoulder. I kiss her clavicle and trace my lips to her shoulder and catch the moment she slips a pinch of powder into my bottle. What the f..?

Gloriana bites my earlobe and growls at my ear.

I adjust my groin again, but no position is comfortable.

There's only one way to eliminate the pain. Short of taking her right here, nothing else will do. But I won't take her yet. I'm unsure of what's going on with her. She slipped powder into my drink.

Is she trying to make me sleep or kill me?

On the steps leading below the deck, Rohan clears his throat. I look over.

He shakes his head. "It's a stimulant."

"A what?"

He snorts, suppressing laughter. "A stimulant."

On my lap, Gloriana freezes, and when I look at her, she's blushing.

"You weren't supposed to know that," she says.

Gently, I pinch her chin. "What do you think I need a stimulant for?"

"Intercourse," she whispers.

Rohan laughs.

"Lass, what makes you think I need a stimulant?"

"Fleur said lycans can't get it up if it's not a full moon."

Fleur needs a male with a firm, twitchy palm. Like me. But I'm taken, so I say, "Fleur has no idea what she's talking about, and I'll prove it to you. Let's get out of here."

Rising with my mate in my arms, I head downstairs, then stop. I arrived on this ship full of lycan pirates, and since I didn't think I'd be shagging my mate this evening, I didn't arrange rooms fit for a shag.

"Find Fleur for me, would you?" I ask Rohan.

As if conjured, Fleur arrives. "Do you need assistance?"

The Summer Fae Court's hospitality is something the fairies take seriously, so when the princess asks if I need assistance, she means it. But the truth is, I will come to regret staying at the Summer Court for any length of time, not to mention the time I'll need to secure our transport back to lycan lands. Rohan is staying for the entire summer, so he won't be able to carry my mate and me back.

"I'll need accommodation," I say.

"You will have it."

"Tonight."

Fleur smiles sweetly, showing me a tiny bit of fang. She's up to no good. I just know it. "Gloriana is settled in a large and comfortable end suite. It can accommodate a pack of lycans for the night." She traces a claw over my chest. "A pack of lycans all at the same time. I'm sure you will find it adequate for you and your ego until we can accommodate the pair of you tomorrow."

"Fine." Gloriana's passed out drunk and snoring on my shoulder. "Take me to her rooms."

Fleur snaps her fingers, and a pair of royal guards in yellow coats escort us to the main portal that leads from the boat into the fairy court.

I hate traveling via portals.

2

GLORIANA

Sharp pain hammers my head.

Groaning, I press the heel of my hand against my temple as if the pressure would ward off the pounding. Barely able to open my blurry eyes, I stumble to the bathroom, then return to my bed immediately, feeling as if I might throw up.

"Marybell," I groan out, and manage to peel open one eye.

A blurry figure stands by the window.

"Marybell," I repeat. "Call the healer."

A snort is her response.

"My head is pounding," I tell my lady-in-waiting. "I need the herbs and the healer."

"What you need," a deep, rough male voice says, "is a hearty spanking."

I screech and sit up in bed, and my stomach lurches. Pressing a hand over my middle, I blink, trying to clear last night's haze, but failing.

The figure standing near the windows is large, bulky, and definitely not Marybell, but I can't make out his face yet.

It takes me a moment to realize I'm alone in my bedchamber with a male I thought was my servant. Is Marybell even here? And what is a male doing in my chambers? Oh no!

My hand flies to my mouth, fingertips tracing my lips, checking for swelling from kissing. "Did we...?" I ask, leaving the rest to dangle, certain the male will know what I'm asking him.

When the male doesn't answer, I realize I'm completely nude. You'd think I would have realized that when I went to the bathroom, but no. I must still be drunk.

I grab a fistful of sheets and pull them to my chin, then draw my knees up to my chest.

A snort comes from him again.

I rub my eyes and roll them a little bit, trying to see straight. "I don't know who you are or what you're doing here, but you need to leave."

"Is this how you treat all yer lovers? Throw them out after a good night of fun? Or do they leave before you awake and Marybell takes over yer care after one too many drinks?"

I've never had lovers. I was a virgin. And who is this male to question what I did? "What I do is not your business. Get out." Too many drinks. What an ass. As if he was sober. Males like to judge females in the Stenan lands, but not as much in the fae lands, especially not in the Summer Court, where everyone is open to way more fun than I've ever had under Father's rule.

A door clicks open, and Marybell's voice drifts in. "How are you feeling, milady?"

"Like a horse ran over me," I say.

A smaller person draws near me and bends, putting what I think is a tray on my nightstand.

"Marybell, I can't seem to blink off the haze from my eyes. Please call the healer." And I'm nauseated.

Fae healing magic is like a miracle. With a single touch, a warm wave sweeps over the body, and all the pains disappear. I wish the healers could heal broken lives.

Or broken royals, at that.

"Princess Fleur said you might have glamour haze. She gave me herbs, and I made you a tea." The bed dips slightly as Marybell takes a seat and brings the tea to my lips.

I take the cup and sip slowly, scrunching up my nose at the odor. "Thank you."

"It smells like crap," Marybell says.

"The herb that clears the glamour," the male says, "is made of mushrooms that grow on aged cow shite. It is crap."

"He's still here," I whisper to Marybell.

"Yes, milady."

"He can hear you," the male says.

"I'd hoped," I whisper to Marybell, "that I'd conjured him up in my head."

"No, milady. He brought you to the chambers last night."

I sip my tea. "I think we had sex."

Marybell says nothing, but her face is becoming clearer. I tip the teacup and pour the contents down my throat, and a flashback of Fleur downing a bottle of nasty hard liquor I couldn't name, then passing me the bottle, comes back from last night. I swigged from it as Fleur told me she would glamour me again tonight. She would hate for anyone to try to take advantage of me because I'm a Stenan and not a fae or another creature of magic.

A Stenan female among the fae stands out.

And a single Stenan female among the fae stirs rumors of the lost Kilseleian princess who my dead father's former soldiers are searching for. Someone must take the blame for the fall of the king and the destruction of the lives that followed.

The miners who worked for my father can't defeat the savages, so they've been coming after me.

The Summer king hid me on his estate and now hides me in his court so I can have a bit of fun at my age. I'm only eighteen and already sequestered on a secluded estate, doomed to spend my life hiding from the enemies my father's centuries of reign have amassed.

Marybell smiles, her kind brown eyes crinkling at the corners.

"I see you now."

"There you are, my lady."

I put down the cup and lean over to the right to see the male, who's still present in my room. He's standing at the white terrace doors now, the curtains already pushed aside to allow light into the room. His back is to me.

From his accent, I don't believe he's fae, but his hair's down, and I can't be sure if he's a Stenan man, with round ears instead of pointy fae ones. Stubble as dark as ink covers some of his throat and reaches above his jaw. The way he stands, with his feet shoulder-width apart and his head turned slightly up, arms crossed over his chest, I presume, makes me feel like he's some sort of guard. Or soldier. A warrior of some sort, for sure.

Broad shoulders, tapered waist.

What's he wearing? At first, it appeared as new fae-fashioned shorts, but I recognize it now as a green-and-black kilt with black boots. I frown. Is the male a lycan? Unlikely. I'm on fae shores.

An uneasy feeling stirs in my belly.

At the end of my father's reign, my father's service males came after me. And so did the lycans, to whom my father promised riches when he defeated the savages. In the aftermath of the battle, which my father lost, a lycan male came forward and claimed I was his mate.

The savages who took over the crown, the city, the entire country I've known as home, agreed to hand me over to the lycan. They didn't care about me, and even though I pleaded with the former queen to help me she said she couldn't stand between the lycan and his mating claim.

The Summer king wouldn't either.

That's why I didn't tell the king about the claim before asking for help.

The male turns and leans against the door.

His arms are crossed over his chest, drawing my gaze toward his abundant muscles that are covered under a white tunic. It's the eyes that give him away. Lycans have the eyes of a wolf. They're often blue, like this male's, and outlined in black ink as if they use makeup.

"Hello, Princess," he says. "Remember me?"

3

GLORIANA

Marybell takes the tray outside. I clutch the sheets. I had sex with a lycan, and no, I don't remember. That's too bad, really, because I've heard lycans are attentive lovers. What to say...what to say...

"Mmhm," I say.

"Mmhm?" he repeats.

"I remember."

He tilts his head. "What do you remember, lass?"

I pick at the white flower embroidered near the hem of the pink silk sheets. "I remember you were a very attentive lover, and I thank you for helping me with my virginity problem."

When he doesn't answer, I peek up at him from under my bangs.

His expression remains impassive. I can't read it. Powerful males tend to have these types of expressions. I call them masks, and because they wear them all their lives, they cannot be trusted.

"Is there anything more?" I ask, trying to give him a hint that he should leave.

"There's much more."

I chew my lip. "I realize this is a bit uncomfortable, but if you would exit with grace, it would make everything more pleasant." I don't want to have to ask him to leave.

He strides to the bed and, instead of leaving, sits next to me.

The scent of fresh-shaven male and chestnuts burning over fire in the winter of an evergreen forest hits me in the rib cage. It makes my heart go aflutter. He smells like… comfort food, and strength. No wonder Fleur chose this lycan for me last night. It's unfortunate I don't remember how he performed in bed.

Blue eyes regard me as if trying to see inside my soul.

He leans in closer and crooks his finger, calling me to meet him halfway.

"I didn't realize yer virginity was a problem that needed solving."

Oh my. His voice is really deep. "I did."

"And you say I was an attentive lover?"

I nod, leaning in some more.

His lips are plush, he smells amazing, and he's hot. Not the fae kind of hot, but more bulky, rough-terrain kind of hot. I want to kiss him.

"If I was an attentive lover, why are you trying to get rid of me now?"

"Because I missed the brunch, which means I have a luncheon to attend."

He blinks as if that makes no sense to him. Maybe it doesn't. I explain. "I take it you are not familiar with the etiquette for attending royal events."

"I know the basics."

"Then you know that if a lady and a male walk in together for a luncheon, they're the couple for the season."

"And you don't wish to couple with me?"

I shake my head. "I'm sorry, I do not."

"Why not?" A whisper over my lips.

I'm so close to kissing him. It's like he's pulling me in, but he's not. He's not even trying. I'm the one who's leaning into him. Also, he's not leaving the chambers, and he must leave the chambers. I should start dressing. Dressing takes time.

"Because I wish to experience as many lovers as possible in the fae court."

He leans back, and now it's my turn to blink. I almost kissed this male. Is he putting me under some sort of spell? I didn't think lycans did magic. They're one of the rare creatures of magic who do not actually perform magic other than shifting from male to wolf.

"I doubt yer wish will come true."

"Why wouldn't it?"

"Because I intend to court you for the season."

"You can't do that. That wasn't part of the deal."

"The deal?"

I nod. "Last night, Fleur said we were going on the lycan pirate ships. When I protested, citing one lycan's mating claim and the risk of being discovered, she said the lycan pirates are business males and don't spread rumors if paid." I pause to allow him to comment.

He motions with a hand. "Please do continue."

"The deal was that I pick a lycan male, lose my virginity, and pay him to forget he ever saw me."

"I take it I'll get paid for sleeping with you?"

"Not for sleeping with me. For silence. Silence is rewarded with coins in the fae lands."

The male scrubs him jaw, nodding. "I'm starting to understand what's happening here."

"Oh, good." He will leave my chambers now.

Granted, I would like him to stay. The lycan who has a mating claim on me was rough and unkempt looking and much older. This male is clean-shaven, presentably dressed, and also older, but in an attractive kind of way.

Standing, he bows and offers me his palm. "Princess."

I place my hand in his, then realize I don't even know his name. "Lycan."

He drops a kiss on my hand, watching me the entire time. Those blue wolf eyes entrap me as I say, "I hope you have a pleasant voyage back home."

He smiles, showing me a bit more of his sharp teeth than I'd like, before striding out of my room.

4

LENOX

The Summer king favors my mate indeed.

The Kilseleian princess's father lost his crown, and yet the Summer king placed Gloriana in one of the most coveted rooms in the courtesans' tower. She's housed at the very top, along with other royalty and the most respected fae females.

This means that when I exit her suite at the end of the corridor, half-dressed courtesans are crossing the hallway, zipping between the rooms and shared spaces. As they spot me over here at the end, looking murderous and determined to kill the Summer king, they stop to giggle.

Soon enough, they've cleared the narrow hallway and are standing at their chamber doors like soldiers at attention, except they carry hairbrushes and are barely dressed in any clothes, let alone a full-body uniform.

I'm the only male here, and this is my walk of shame.

I pull back my shoulders and march down the hallway as if two dozen or so fairies aren't giggling and whispering about the size of my shoulders, my shaven jaw, and the Alpha lycan scent I leave in my wake.

My fae is rusty, but as I understand it, my scent pleases the fae females. It should also please my mate, the one the scent is intended for, except I doubt her sense of smell is strong enough to detect it.

Unlike the fae, we lycans don't release the scent whenever we please. Once we have a mate, the scent is always present to attract our mate. Every male smells his own unique way, and an Alpha male's scent is always more potent than that of a beta male.

Our scent is designed by nature to attract a submissive mate. It also attracts other submissive females, and if a male attracts fairies in the Summer Court, the male attracts attention of the highest order.

The whistling and hooting starts as I near the middle of the hallway.

"Will you be coming to the luncheon?" one fairy asks.

"Certainly." I pick up my pace.

"I shall look for you, lycan."

"I'm already taken, I'm afraid."

"Already dumped, more like it."

The females laugh.

Ouch. Should've made a run for the exit.

The moment the grand doors close behind me, the heat of the summer hits me right in my sensitive eyes. I narrow them and shield them with a hand, blocking the sun's rays.

The atrium's nearly empty, but a guard or two walk about. I approach one and ask, "Where is the luncheon being held?"

"At Jean's cliffs." He points to a set of rocks jutting from the sea and leaning out over the water. It looks like it used to be a part of the land, but water eventually surrounded it.

"It seems far," I say.

"We have portals," he reminds me. "Nothing is far."

Right. I hate those things.

"Can you get there by boat?" I ask.

"If you can climb the steep cliff, you can access the luncheon from the boat."

Sounds better than portal travel. I nod at the male and stroll out of the atrium, through the hallways, across multiple squares and across long bridges, to finally arrive at the shore from which I row my small boat to Rohan's pirate ship.

There, I grab a sun hat and some ale and lean against the bar, not too far from the comfortable place where my princess and I sat last night.

She was all over me, having no clue we're mates, and woke up thinking she took me to bed so I could bleed her. If I hadn't expected such a charade from the likes of Fleur, I would be offended.

Rohan climbs up from the lower deck, wiping his hands on a dirty rag. He tosses the rag behind the bar and pours an ale.

His blue eyes crinkle at the corners. "It's too sunny to brood." He drinks the ale, his throat moving quickly.

I match his speed and pour us another. "I'm not brooding."

"Good. I'd hate to think that you've become your uncle over the turns."

I hated my uncle and often wonder why I've kept him around for as long as I have. My uncle was Rohan's dad, though Rohan rarely called him that.

"I haven't become him, and I'm not brooding."

"What do you call what you're doing?"

"Intellecting."

"That requires a brain."

"You're so funny."

He laughs at his joke and winks. "What's the thought of the span?"

"I'm trying to figure out how to best handle the situation with my mate."

He nods. "And how will you handle it?"

In the distance, the three cliffs are lined up one next to another, with the largest in the middle, reminding me of a cock and balls. Go figure, the fairies would have a male package sticking out right at the front of their court.

"She thinks we mated last night."

"Last night?" Rohan asks. "But she passed out while you two were still on the ship."

I nod. "I was an attentive lover, she said, and it was her first time."

Rohan snorts, and the ale shoots down his windpipe, making him cough and laugh at the same time.

"Choke and die, arsehole." I go behind the bar and find a clean rag. "Here, wipe yer beard."

Rohan takes the rag and mops up. His blue eyes lift at the corners. "Let me guess."

I raise a palm. "No, thank you."

"I'm gonna guess anyway. Ye took her to her chambers and put her in bed. Then you shifted and slept in the corner like a good big wolf."

Dick. "Not in the corner." I sprawled out in the middle of the room, one eye on the door, wondering if anyone would come in, praying the Summer king would arrive and I'd have an excuse to rip his guts out with my teeth.

Rohan throws back his head and laughs.

I want to punch him in the throat, but that would crush his windpipe and kill him, so I don't. Crossing my arms, I eye the cliffs, where the staff are starting to set up the tents for the luncheon. Water surrounds the cliffs on all sides. It's almost like a mini island, a strange piece of land with a strange structure right off the shore.

"Are you done laughing now?" I ask.

"For now. Surely you'll do something stupid while you court her for the summer, and I'll laugh some more."

"Court her?" I snort. "I'm not gonna court her. She's my mate. Therefore, she already belongs to me."

"Is that why she ran away?"

I grab the back of his neck and slam his head against the bar.

Rohan jabs my belly, and I bend over, releasing him at the same time. He throws an uppercut as if to hit my jaw, but I straighten and hurl myself at him. We wrestle on the deck, throwing punches left and right. My lip's bleeding, and the taste of blood makes me want to shift and rip into Rohan.

I'm sure he feels the same way.

But not all blood tastes the same. His is that of a friend, not a foe or even prey, and a hearty brawl with my cousin is just what I needed.

My mating claim went unanswered for far too many cycles, and the waiting is catching up with me, my wolf growing more aggressive in its desire to mark Gloriana's neck and calm the fuck down.

And since I won't take my mate by force, it means I might actually have to court her.

I pin Rohan to the deck. "Fine, I'll court her."

"Naturally," a male voice says.

I snap my head around and groan when I see who caught us fighting. The Summer king himself. Rolling off Rohan, I get up and offer my cousin a hand. He fixes his tattered clothes and bows at the waist, blood dripping on the deck.

The king acknowledges the greeting with a tilt of his head.

For my greeting, I nod, having already bowed once a few nights ago when I confronted him about hiding my mate.

King Et'enne stands as tall as me, with narrower shoulders and a slender, refined build. His black hair is pulled back in a tight bun at the top of his head and secured by sticks which I hear end in blades hidden in his hair. He wears black on black with golden bands around his wrists, matching his golden shoes.

I'd rather die than wear golden shoes. That's all I have to say about the Summer king.

"My future queen is with me. You may wish to clean up before she comes on board."

Rohan and I exchange looks. His smirk tells me exactly how he intends to clean up. He picks up the hem of his ripped shirt and yanks it off his body. The kilt is next, and since he's barefoot, all that's left to do is to run across the deck and jump into the sea.

A lady wearing a black veil over her face ascends from the lower deck, but pauses when she sees I'm undressing.

Nude, and with my half erection dangling between my legs, I wink at the king. "Yer court, yer rules. I'm cleaning up." I jump into the water.

Rohan's trying not to choke on laughter as we use the ladder to get back onto the lower deck. We wrap towels around our hips before climbing the stairs to the upper deck, where we find the king pinning his female against the bar.

The fae are in their mating season, and even the king has urges.

We give them a moment and sit in the same seats we occupied last night. Soon, they join us. I expect the female to remove the black veil she wears, but she keeps it on. I've heard she is a fae fate, one of three females the fae regard as divinity. The lycans don't share the same culture or language with the fae.

Besides being born with magic, we have very little in common with the fae.

And even less with Kilseleians and Stenans, which are my mate's predecessors.

The king takes the future queen's hand. They sit to our right, and when the summer breeze blows our way, both Rohan and I can't stop our instincts. We turn up our noses and flare our nostrils to inhale the scent of the Summer female's arousal.

By my hairy balls, she smells pleasant and conjures up images of a submissive female, all cute shyness and willingness to please me in bed. Gloriana's face comes to mind. I envision her on her knees with a mouth full of cum, her eyes looking up at me, seeking both mercy and a hard shag.

Rohan whacks the back of my head. "Stop rumbling."

I whack him back. "Fine."

The king clears his throat. "My June enjoyed looking at the lycan males' bodies, and I'll reap the benefits of that. However, if you present yourself to her again, I'll be forced to rip off your balls and feed them to you. Do I make myself fucking clear?"

I smile. We pissed off the Summer king. He lost the temper he holds on to for dear life. It's nice to push his buttons. I want to do it more often, only perhaps not in the presence of his future queen.

"Do I?" he asks.

"Yes, Your Majesty," Rohan says, and I nod.

"What can we do for you?" Rohan asks.

"Several things." The female passes him a drink. The bubbly wine the fairies prefer, not our ale.

"Gloriana is my first concern."

I can barely stand him saying her name with his musical male voice and his pretty accent.

He smiles, showing me a fang. "Gloriana is like a sister to me." The way he says her name is sensual, and I have a feeling he's saying it in a way that makes it sexy on purpose just to piss me off.

A growl builds in my chest.

In our native tongue, Rohan says, "What the fuck is wrong with you?"

"I hate how he's saying my mate's name. As if he's eating pussy and loving it."

"He's the Summer king. Every word out of his mouth sounds like he's eating fine royal pussy. They're in mating season, and we need to keep our wits about us."

I nod. He's right. I came with him, on his ships, and brought none of my males, as was the deal. Too many lycans following two Alphas in a confined space for any length of time spells fighting and dead males. I boarded his ship alone.

Alone also means I don't have the show of force I would have with my entire clan, and the fairies do love a show of power. I can't bow to the Summer king, but I also can't deliberately provoke or disrespect him. After all, he has been kind and hospitable to me.

"Yer hospitality is appreciated, Your Majesty," I say. "But Gloriana is no longer yer concern. She is my mate."

"So you say." With a slight tilt of his head to the future queen, a surge of magic rises, along with the hair at the back of my neck. The king nods. "And now, I believe you."

"What the hell was that?" I ask Rohan in lycan.

"The magic of the fate." The female speaks for the first time, her voice like a butterfly landing atop my dick.

"I mean no offense," she says in lycan. "My visions come and go of their own volition. I merely saw the moment you realized the girl is yours. It was outside on a rainy day and four turns ago, when Gloriana returned from riding one morning. You were in wolf form and carrying some prey you'd caught in the forest. A full-grown boar, I believe." The fairy smiles as she recalls one of my favorite memories. "You didn't claim her then. You returned when she grew older."

I shift in my seat, the female fate making me uncomfortable. I dislike knowing she can see that memory. It feels intrusive since nobody else knows about it. "That's right."

"The circumstances at the time of Gloriana's asking my assistance guided my decision to take her and put her somewhere safe. Had I known she was a lycan's mate, I would have ensured your claim before I allowed you to have her."

"Allowed me to have her?" I lean in. "I don't need yer permission to have my mate."

"That's not what I meant," the Summer king says. "Hear me out. The savages killed her father and took over his court. When she asked for shelter, I was not aware of your claim."

I don't know if I believe him, but it matters not right now. I'm at his court, and I hate feeling as if I'm at his mercy.

The king tilts his head. "My court is a mating playground, and guests are welcome to play," he says as if addressing what I'm thinking. That's impossible, but I need to remain on guard. I hate dealing with fairies.

"Now that you're aware of my claim, you will offer me yer hospitality and space for my claiming."

"Certainly. But might I remind you of the customs in the

Summer Court? We seduce females, Mr. McMar. It is an art and makes for fun and pleasure."

"I have a distinct feeling you think me a brute and unable to woo a female."

"I simply came here to remind you that Gloriana is protected, even if she is no longer a crown princess. I would see her made happy, and I'm sure you're the male who can do that."

"I'm sure I am the only male who can."

"The pirate boats are hardly a place to mate," he says.

"I couldn't agree with you more."

"You will have the family guest suites in my tower," the future queen says.

"Yer tower?"

"I know. It's hard to believe I have a tower, isn't it?"

Frowning, I try to puzzle out what the fairy is saying. Why would it be hard to believe the king's chosen has a tower?

"I come from a family of farmers." She points toward the mountains. "Up there. And now I have a tower."

"And now I have the entire clan," I say, realizing the future queen can see things about me I wish nobody could. The reference to her farm life is a direct relation to my past. The future queen and I might be kindred souls as much as the king and Gloriana are. They grew up having everything. His female and I grew up having nothing.

Somehow, I have earned favor with the future Summer queen.

I smile my sexiest smile and rise so I can bow deeply before her. I don't rise back up, so she will have to offer me her hand. When she does, I brush my lips over her skin, and because I'm a lycan male in mating, my scent is strong and hearty.

As I rise, the female picks up her handheld fan and flares it out.

"You toy with your life, lycan," the king says.

Rohan pokes my ribs with his elbow. "The deck is yours for as long as you wish to use it, milady."

The king smirks and throws an arm over the back of the future queen's seat. "Let my brother know if you need something in the tower. And lycan," the king says, "you should know that Gloriana's inheritance makes her a target for several Kilseleian males who were in the service of the dead king. This is the reason she resides in my court. When you take her, you must become familiar with the threats surrounding the princess."

"I'll kill anyone who stands in the way of my claim on my mate."

"No doubt. The princess knows their names. When you've claimed her and have her trust, I'm sure she will share the names with you."

"Or you could give them to me now."

"I could."

I wait, but the king sets down his drink and then turns toward his female. Her arousal flares in the air as he releases his scent, I presume to drown out mine.

Rohan and I descend the steps and stop at the rail on the lower deck.

My cousin grips the rail. "He wants something in return for the information on the people who are a threat to your mate."

I snort. "I wondered how long it would take for him to beat around the bush before the real reason why he came out here."

"He does care about the princess."

"I'm sure. But he will also try to gain access to lycan trade routes via said princess."

Rohan nods. "We need a plan."

"On how to scale the cliffs."

"What?"

"The cliffs." I point at the place where the luncheon will be held. "We're gonna scale them."

"Why would we do that?"

"Because it'll get us laid."

A light comes on for Rohan. I can see it in his eyes. "This is your idea of romance."

"Damn straight it is." Bare-chested lycan males working up a sweat are what wet dreams are made of.

5

GLORIANA

Marybell rubs oil on my shoulders while I stand at the mirror with long brown hair extensions covering my breasts. I'm trying to decide if I like my new hair extensions enough to keep them or if I'll go out without them.

I catch Marybell's eye in the mirror.

"What do you think of my new hairstyle?"

"It's pretty."

"Hmmm. Is it prettier than the old one?" I cut my hair recently. Chin length and with bangs was the style I arrived to court with. Fleur ordered extensions for last night to see how they look.

"It depends."

"On?"

"What the lycan male who was here this morning thinks."

I smile. "He was handsome, wasn't he?"

She nods. "Wavy black hair. Blue eyes. Muscles the size of a mountain."

I curl my hair around my finger. "Do you think a woman should care what a man thinks of her hair?"

"If she's trying to get his attention, then yes, milady."

"Why should I care?"

"Because you want a repeat of last night, I presume."

"I can't remember last night."

Marybell walks to the water bucket and washes her hands before rolling in the portable hanger that holds several dresses for me to pick from for the luncheon.

"You may not remember last night, but you remember this morning. He was handsome and interested."

"He left my chambers with no reservation."

Marybell scoffs. "Rude." She shrugs. "His loss. You will have fae males to choose from at the luncheon."

Interacting with fae males during summer and not having to tie myself to one sounds great.

I sift through the dresses on the rack and pick up a purple one. No. The shade reminds me of Father's court. I grab a yellow sundress, which is one of the Summer Court's colors, but think not again. I wore yellow yesterday afternoon.

The other dresses are royal blue, the color of the season.

Sighing, I sit on the bed. "I have nothing to wear."

"Right," Marybell says, her voice flat.

"But I have to wear something."

"Do you?"

We giggle. In the Summer Fae Court during mating season, clothing is optional, treated as an accessory for the bodies of the fae people.

"Speaking of lycans, we have some lycan fashions."

I sit up. "Like what?"

"Remember the chest of clothes the lycan who wanted to mate you brought as a gift?" When I nod, Marybell continues. "When you said to leave the chest at the Kilseleian court, I opened it and kept a few pieces. I figured I'd wear them, but they're yours to take, milady."

"I won't wear things you like enough to keep. You never keep anything."

"These are...more my style." Marybell averts her gaze.

"How so?"

Marybell looks up at the ceiling as if searching for a word. "They cover more skin."

"Ah. The old court style." My father's Kilseleian court, which I refer to as the old court, was moderate, and usually, I wore long dresses with sleeves covering my shoulders. Granted, my father had no problem parading my body on display for the savage he wished to marry me off to. When the savage male arrived, Father made me wear a white summer dress that scarcely covered my bare mound.

My father knew the lycan had already claimed me as his mate and was on his way to get me, so by marrying me off to a savage, my father would have the lycans solve his savage problem. Upon docking at our shores and discovering that the savage had taken me, the lycan Alpha would attack the horde.

While savages possess powerful magic, lycans are fierce fighters on the open field, and with their aid, my father's court would withstand the savage horde attack.

His plan failed. He lost his life and I lost my tiara, the thing that made me a prospect for marrying El'jah, the Summer Court's prince. While El'jah could never be faithful and also invited males into his bedchamber, the marriage would further cement the alliance between the fae and Kilseleians.

But look at me now.

Hunted. Powerless. Alone.

Marybell returns from the adjacent room where she sleeps, several dresses folded over her arm.

I rub the fabric and realize it's wool. "These are cold-weather clothes."

"One would think, but look." She lays the clothes out on the bed.

There are two outfits.

One of them is a simple green dress with a red wool jacket cut high under the breast. Marybell starts removing the sleeves. Paired with the deep green dress, the two appear...unusual.

"I'll wear it."

After Marybell helps me dress, I walk back to the mirror. The green color is rich and bold, and I like it. "Do you know the name of this color?" I lift the dress above my knee. "There. That's better."

"Deep pine green, milady." Marybell starts pinning the dress for the quick trim.

"A little higher yet."

Marybell lifts the dress to midthigh.

I nod, happy with the length.

My hair covers the red jacket, so I hold it up, then twist it into a high bun.

"The dress complements your eyes."

My hazel eyes appear green now. I approach the mirror and stare at my reflection. "If you are not the Kilseleian princess, then who are you?"

Born and raised a princess who would one day marry a prince, I was spoiled and taught the art of court etiquette and how to best attract a respectable prince. I guarded my virginity, my privacy, and never once even entertained the idea of being anything other than a princess.

Then the savages barged into my court and destroyed it along with my identity.

"You are my lady," Marybell says softly.

I blink back the tears accumulating in my eyes. "Thank you."

She curtsies and helps me out of the dress so she can trim it before I wear it.

After Father lost his crown, and his life, I lost my position in society, my calling in life. As I'd been raised for the purpose of marrying to expand and strengthen Father's power, my governesses taught me several languages and made me read about different cultures, but otherwise, I lived sequestered and hidden away, much the same way the Summer King had hidden me on an estate in the court.

The estate, while vast, was boring, and I pleaded with the king to let me come to court for the season. I wanted a taste of freedom. I wanted a male who would ravage me and make me scream the way I heard kitchen maids scream when Father's soldiers came back to town.

At first, the Summer king refused, citing concerns for my safety, but recently, he sent a carriage and brought me to court. Under one condition. That I wear glamour and appear as a fairy.

My father made lots of promises he didn't keep, and some of his partners will want a pound of his flesh.

I'm the only flesh they can get.

The excited squealing of fairy females down the hall lures me to walk toward the doors, and as I'm about to press my ear against the wood, the doors swing open. The pair of royal guards announce El'jah, the Summer Court's prince.

What's he doing in my chambers?

6

GLORIANA

El'jah is a tall blue-eyed blond with sun-kissed skin and a smile that melts icebergs. He's incorporating savage styles into fae fashions and wearing jewelry in his hair and around his wrists. He wears no fur or heavy materials like savages do, but the leather pants with five belts around his waist, a black shirt, and rings on his fingers make him appear dangerous.

His scent, that of a male fairy, a mix of sea and shells, salty and flowery, yet masculine, enters my nose as he bends to kiss my cheek. My nipples perk, and I suppress a moan, remembering I cannot have this male, even though I harbor confusing fantasies about him.

Judging by the groups of ladies hovering by my door, most people in the Summer Court fantasize about the prince. Even more so now that a female snapped up the Summer king, leaving the prince as the most eligible bachelor.

El'jah looks me up and down, tiny flecks of magic dancing in his eyes. I'm happy to see he finds my body attractive, though I shyly cover my breasts. "You shouldn't be here while I'm dressing," I say.

The guards stand at the door and allow everyone to see inside. This is for my benefit. El'jah and I shouldn't be alone in my chambers, but since I've lost my tiara, my virginity, and my identity, what's a lost reputation, hm?

For some reason, El'jah wants to preserve my reputation.

"I wouldn't be here if you weren't running late." He looks around. "Where's that sexy thing of yours? Mary!" He snaps his fingers, making the stacks of bracelets on his wrist jingle.

Marybell bursts into the room and holds up the green dress. I put it on, and it fits me perfectly, the length adjusted to reach midthigh. I sling on the red jacket. Curling my toes, I'm considering what sandals to pick out when Marybell slides me a pair of open-toe black summer boots.

They're leather and rise all the way to my thigh.

"Won't I be hot in them?" I ask.

El'jah points at his leather pants. "The elves on staff have been instructed to make the breeze colder than usual." He offers me his elbow, and I place a gentle hand on it before he walks me out of my room. If we arrive at the luncheon together, people will consider us a couple for the season.

Powerless and no longer a princess, I'm not being courted by El'jah. I'm unsure what he's doing, but I can't refuse the Summer prince. This family is all I have in terms of protection from people hunting me for my father's sins.

As we walk down the hallway of the courtesans' tower, filled with fae staying here for the season, females in every state of undress stand at the doors of their rooms to be seen by the prince. Passing, he smiles and makes eye contact with each of them.

El'jah is hot and attentive, really knows how to court a girl.

"A certain lycan walked the walk of shame this morning, I hear."

Heat spreads over my cheeks just as the guards open the exit doors.

El'jah stops before the portal. "On a scale from one to twelve, with twelve being reserved for a ménage à trois with a girl and a boy, how was the lycan Alpha?"

I shrug.

Elijah's eyes widen. "A seven? Only?"

I shake my head.

He gasps. "Average. A five?"

"I can't remember."

His shocked expression makes me laugh.

El'jah peeks under the collar of my jacket. "You're not even marked."

"Is that a bad thing?"

He appears confused. "It depends."

"I'm starting to hate that answer."

The prince jerks his head toward the portal, and we walk through the shimmering green magic to appear on the grass atop the cliff right off the Summer Court's shores. Despite the sultry music encouraging the mingling of horny fae, and the pixies offering hors d'oeuvres and drinks, nobody is on the lawn. They're all gathered at the other end of the cliff as if trying to peer off the edge.

"Looks like something's going on," I say.

I snatch a champagne flute while El'jah grabs my other hand and pulls me toward the edge.

As we reach the back of the crowds, El'jah whispers, "Excuse us."

Though their backs are to us, the crowd of about three hundred parts instantly.

The fae prince's magic is something of a mystery, and he likes to keep it that way. Rumors have it he's a *voca*, a creature who can manipulate minds. Based on this small display of power, I believe the rumors.

We walk to the edge of the cliff and peer down the steep decline.

A single small white boat carrying two males floats over the soft waves toward the cliff. As it approaches, pale yellow magic sparkles around the males, and in an instant, they stand taller and larger, with furry wolflike faces and massive, clawed, hairy hands.

The crowd gasps as if they've never seen anything like it before. I'm glad I'm not the only one.

"I thought lycans were large wolves," I say.

"Lycans are triform creatures. A male, a wolf, and this middle form called a werewolf. If you see this form, you're probably dead since they use it in combat."

"Um, that can't be good." Since they're here and in that form.

Face partially covered in dark fur tipped in silver with a nose extended into a muzzle to accommodate the growth of long, sharp, predatory teeth, the male who took me last night is scanning the crowd, his blue eyes glowing with the magic of a werewolf.

I can't help feeling as if he's looking for me.

El'jah whistles and raises our joined hands, waving them in the air.

"Here, puppy!" he shouts. "Come get your treat."

The male snaps his gaze our way and peels back his lips, showing us his dark gums and long, sharp, flesh-tearing canines right before he crouches and executes an impossibly high leap.

He slams his body against the stone cliff.

The other male follows.

I lean farther over the edge, but can't see them because of the steep inward angle from up here. This means they're climbing with their backs almost horizontal to the seas.

"They're gonna fall," I say.

"Maybe," El'jah says.

"Why would anyone do this?"

"To show you his masculine skills."

"What for? Oh! He did say he intended to court me."

El'jah chews his nail, clearly a nervous gesture. A lycan falling off the cliff to his death would upset the fine cheer in the court, and the fae would hate to cut short the festivities to mourn for even a single span.

"Since you can't remember him in the bedroom," El'jah says, "he's compensating."

I hadn't considered that he'd scale a steep overhang trying to impress me. "Surely that's not it. I'm not difficult to impress."

"That may be so, but I was shocked to learn he walked away from your chambers this morning. Even more surprised you're unmarked. What did you say to him?"

"I said thank you." El'jah keeps mentioning markings. Some fae males bite females during mating. Others even bruise them. It is a sign of great affection, and the females wear the markings proudly, even adjusting their clothes so that the bruising or tooth marks show.

El'jah laughs. "No wonder he's scaling the cliff. *Thanks*," he mimics my girly voice. "*Bye, lycan*."

I chuckle. "It wasn't like that." It was.

The prince shakes his head. "You wounded his pride, and he wants to show you he's worthy of remembering."

"How do you know all this about him? Is he a friend of yours?"

El'jah shakes his head again. "Haven't met him yet."

"Then how do you know he's climbing to impress me?" I watch El'jah's profile, noting a brief flare of magic in the corner of his eye.

"I have a knack for knowing what people want."

He tilts his head, then turns toward the crowd and whispers, "The lycans will emerge." This soft yet firm tone of voice, an enticing melody, almost feels like he's asking me for a favor I can't refuse.

"Of course they will, Prince El'jah." I'm compelled to answer, even though I don't want to.

"Stop worrying," he whispers. "Cheer them on."

"Come on!" a fairy female shouts. "I have a purse of coins bet on the taller one."

The others whistle and hoot, and soon, the crowd is encouraging the lycans to emerge over the rock that's blocking the view.

And they do.

On the far right, a huge clawed hand slams over the top rock, and the lycan's body follows, swinging up, landing in a crouch. The taller wolf snaps his head up and leaps again, propelling himself through the air, a blur of muscle and power.

Delighted at the display of agility, the fairies are screaming, and when the male lands on the grass near us, cheers erupt.

The females surround him.

Many beautiful fairies with their enticing mating scents a lycan nose detects with no trouble. They're stroking his muscles, petting the wolf's fur around the male's shoulders, and even daring to rub behind his ears. Since the male is the tallest person in the gathering, his blue-eyed gaze blazes past everyone's heads right to where El'jah and I stand.

Blushing, I wave, saying hello again.

The male makes his way toward us, and I recall something El'jah said. "What did you mean by unmarked. What mark?"

El'jah pats my head. "Oh, you poor clueless virgin."

"Is that..." My voice trails off, and I start backing away.

As the lycan marches forward, he lifts his hands palm up. "Ain't gonna hurt you, lass."

"I think you have a runner, wolf," El'jah says, then turns to me and slaps my behind. Magic flares in his blue eyes. Voice soft and persuasive, he whispers, "Run."

I turn and sprint as fast as my legs can carry me.

7
LENOX

What we lack in magical abilities, we make up for in raw strength, and strength is a form of power. Since power is everything in the fae court, I figured I would show my mate mine.

Climbing the slippery angled incline was a difficult and trying feat that both Rohan and I executed flawlessly and with a speed the fairies can only dream of. On top of that, we scaled the incline in our werewolf form, the form that demands the most energy since we occupy a single body as both the wolf and the male.

Proud of my accomplishment and sure it impressed my mate, I swagger toward her, expecting a hug, a kiss, a dick lick, whatever I can get. I'm not picky.

She spins and runs.

Now, I am an Alpha male werewolf out here in the fairyland, trying to claim my mate who ran from me once before. I have been dousing my instincts, placating my wolf, jerking off till my knob's raw for about half a dozen full moons. Frankly, I'm feeling rejected by a female who should, by the laws of nature, submit to me easily.

Before I can stop, my wolf snarls and ignites the full transition. Yellow magic flares, taking me from male to wolf, and on four legs, I take off after the Kilseleian princess as if someone lit my tail on fire. She sprints down the row of tables and reaches the other end of the cliff. I can't have her jumping into the portal. A million thoughts race through my mind.

What if she misses the portal and falls?

Would she jump to get away from me?

Am I that repulsive to her?

It matters not right now. In wolf form, I stand as tall as she, and I'm faster than most creatures in the world, which means I close the distance quickly and tackle her. Under me on the grass, she starts screaming and struggling, which provokes my claiming instinct.

I close my jaw on the back of her neck and growl, a warning for her to stop thrashing.

One of my sharp fangs pierces her skin, and her blood coats my tongue, igniting the claiming magic that calms me, sates the need for marking my mate.

The mark allows me control over my mind and magic so I can transition from wolf back into a male. As a male, I pin her down by holding her shoulders to discourage moving and bite down a little harder, piercing her skin more, marking her neck, marking the female as mine.

Her soft whimper makes me harden between the legs. I lick her wounds until they're closed and healed, but the scars will remain on her skin forever.

Mine. The Kilseleian princess is finally mine.

Breathing hard as if I labored for spans on end, I kiss her cheek, then roll over and sit beside her. Before me, hundreds of gathered fairies watch us, and more fairies are pouring out of the portal behind me. They're staring.

Nobody loves a spectacle more than fairies. If it involves a couple, then it's sure to attract crowds around here. A lycan Alpha coming onto fairy shores and claiming a Kilseleian princess by throwing her on the ground and biting her during luncheon will provide gossip for at least a few spans.

They're whispering and pointing, and that's making me feel like a pet in a cage, something to be observed and played with for their amusement. It's starting to get on my nerves, but I'm trying not to kill anyone while courting a gentle female not of lycan origin.

The princess is still lying on her belly, her gaze on the portal, her lips slightly parted.

I rise and offer her my hand.

The female turns her head, then sits up and takes my hand. Standing, she fixes her clothes and hair, then pierces me with a glare.

Uh-oh. Bad wolf. I can tell she's about to lay it on me. I have a younger sister. I can predict these things.

Standing with my feet shoulder-width apart, I square my shoulders and crack my neck.

I'm ready. Bring it on, female!

The princess curtsies, glaring at me from beneath her bangs. "Enjoy your luncheon."

8

GLORIANA

My father rarely missed an opportunity to bond with me in a way that assured me he intended to help me with my purpose in life. Which was to marry well. Marrying well meant securing an alliance that would give him more power. He never hid his bids for power, the hunger for power I could never understand.

But I understand power and the fact that I have none.

Now more than ever.

Now that the lycan male marked me.

I'm uncertain what it means to be a wolf's mate, but judging by how he handled my attempt to flee, it means he's not letting me go.

I'm back to where I was with my father. Trapped yet again.

Defeated, I start walking away, but the lycan snatches my wrist and pulls me against his body. It's a hard, sweaty male body with a musky scent that I want to lick off the strong jaw that's already showing the shadow of a dark beard.

"Where are you going?" he barks, throwing me off the temporary-madness train. The one that made me want to rise on my toes and angle my face toward that jaw.

"Wherever I damn well please." Tears accumulate in my eyes, and I press my lips together as if that'll help me stitch myself back together. I tug my hand, but he's not letting go, though his blue eyes lose the magical glow, and he blinks as if clearing out the haze.

"I never wish to hurt my mate," he says, "and it hasn't occurred to me until this moment that I might have. I will make it up to you."

I'm not in pain or hurt by him, necessarily. I am defeated and embarrassed, and I find it touching, albeit late, that he cares. It tells me the brute can be sweet.

He continues, "The bite has hurt you, and I will make up for that, but know this. I won't apologize for claiming you."

No, he can't be sweet. "I'm hungry." I don't want to talk about this now. I want to eat and drink and pretend nothing happened until I figure out how to deal with my situation.

The male narrows his eyes. "A lycan female would welcome the claiming of an Alpha male. The claim gives her security and position in the clan."

"I'm not a wolf."

"Even so, I regret nothing. It is my right to mark my mate."

"And what of my rights?!"

He frowns. "I'm unclear what you mean."

"Of course you are, lycan." I snort, an unladylike sound. "Because you do whatever pleases you."

The fairies giggle, eavesdropping on us. I hate arguing, and I hate him for not caring that everyone is listening.

"My mate's happiness pleases me. Of all the creatures of

this world, the wolves are the most attentive and loyal. Make no mistake, lass, I intend to satisfy you."

"That might be so, but you can't throw me down in the dirt and bite me." I poke his chest. "In front of all these people."

"Would you like it better if it were a private affair?" he asks. "Because the marking is a warm-up. I still get to claim you."

He reaches for a lock of my hair.

I slap his hand.

Ignoring my slap, he reaches for my hair again.

I step back.

"Come here, lovers," the prince calls from the table. "Before the wine gets warm and the food gets cold."

I leave the lycan and sit beside El'jah as I normally would. It's the royal table, and I'm the court's guest. The fairies start taking their seats, and as the seating area fills, it becomes obvious there's no place for the wolf at the royal table.

The lycan realizes it too as he approaches, and he has eyes only for El'jah, who stares back as if daring the lycan to rearrange the host's table.

He wouldn't.

Nobody would.

Except for the lycan.

He rounds the table and picks me up off the chair so he can sit in it and plop my bottom on his lap.

Everyone stares at the prince, expecting him to sort out the seating arrangements, while heat crawls up my cheeks at the terribly raw lycan manners.

Next to us, El'jah pretends as if nothing is amiss and even orders ale from the pixies, a clear nod toward the wolf male, a gesture saying the wolf is welcome at the table. In summary, El'jah told the wolf the male is welcome to do what he wants with me and that the Summer fae won't stand in his way.

I'm on my own.

I've never been on my own.

It's terrifying.

9
GLORIANA

Wearing only a bathing suit, the pixie serving our table flips her long purple hair over her matching wings before landing on the lycan's shoulder. A bell chimes as she speaks, and since very few people speak pixie, both the lycan and I count on El'jah for translation.

The prince answers, and they speak back and forth.

"Shodia is disappointed you mated," the prince says.

The lycan throws back his head and laughs.

The pixie joins him, her voice like a wind chime, soft and cute.

"Do you know her?" I ask, wondering why she didn't bring him the ordered ale when she served everyone else wine and champagne.

The lycan nods. "Met her at the boat last night."

My heart starts pounding, and heat returns to my cheeks. I want to throttle the pixie. Her little voice starts annoying me. The lycan spent the night with me, so why is she flirting with him now? More importantly, why do I care?

I flare out the silky black cloth napkin and place it over my lap.

The lycan picks up my fork and taps the plate to get the food-serving pixie's attention.

This pixie, dressed in a miniskirt and a loose white top, flies over, batting her eyelashes at the wolf.

Shodia screeches, and the pixie that just flew over startles and flits away.

"Baby, what do you like?" the wolf asks. He leans forward, his chest pressing against my back. He extends his long arms around me, those magnificent biceps flexing as he pulls the large serving plate the roasted pig is on toward us. He leaves it right in front of him.

The fairies are staring again, but the lycan doesn't care that he stole the main course right out from under their noses.

"After the wolf hunt, and often after mating, the Alpha eats first," El'jah announces to explain the lycan's table manners.

The wolf picks up the carving knife, stabs the roasted piglet, and commences carving the meat and piling it on the plate in front of us.

"Is that enough?" he asks at my ear. The deep rumbling voice makes my clitoris pulse.

On his lap, under the table, I cross one leg over the other and nod.

"Answer me, Princess."

"Yes, wolf."

His lips touch the side of my neck, and I remember the span when we ate with the savages. The span after they conquered Kilselei, and the lycan sat at the long table with the savage males. He piled my plate just the same and fed me. If it weren't for the Summer king joining us and taking me with him after, I'd have spent the last few cycles in the lycan lands. In the lycan clan.

As if I'm a child, the male shifts me on his lap so I'm sitting sideways, my back to El'jah.

Which is ill-mannered.

I shake my head and sit sideways on his lap, the way he wants me to, but facing the prince. The wolf doesn't look happy about it, but proceeds to feed me pork and potatoes.

"I'm eating first," I say.

The wolf nods. "Because the Alpha male is courting you."

"I need a fan." El'jah snatches one from the fairy next to him. He flares it out and starts cooling his face. "I want a wolf too."

"An Alpha is not a toy to want, little prince."

"Oh, please, I don't want an Alpha wolf. I want a wolfy I can toy with."

Images of El'jah with another male ignite an inferno in my channel, and I shift on the wolf's lap. As the lycan feeds me, I lick the pork and potato fat from his fingers. Beneath my thigh, his cock becomes a hard rod, and the blue of his eyes takes on a dim glow.

"Where is your ale?" I ask him as I pick up the champagne glass El'jah keeps refilling for me. Boy, it's getting hot at the table.

"He won't drink it, so Shodia didn't bring it," El'jah answers.

The wolf nods. "That's right."

"Why not?" I ask.

"Because it's from Clan Ott, and I'm from Clan McMar." He says that as if it should mean something to me.

"Unfortunately, I'm unfamiliar with lycan clans."

The wolf scrubs his beard. "I'll teach you about them."

"When?" El'jah interjects.

"Whenever I please."

"She must know about your territorial wars before you take her home with you."

"That is none of yer business, fairy."

"The princess is under the protection of the Summer Court."

The lycan is growling now. "Gloriana is mine."

El'jah pops open a bottle of something I can't identify and pours two shooters. He passes the wolf one, daring him to refuse. The wolf accepts and the males pour the drinks down each other's throats.

Coughing ensues, the males clearly overwhelmed by the rough liquor. What's in the bottle?

I pick up the shooter glass and sniff. It smells strong. No wonder they're coughing.

"She is yours," El'jah says, two fingers flicking at the pixie, who pours another set of shooters. El'jah gives his glass to Shodia, while the wolf offers me his. I accept the shooter and bring it to my lips, but the wolf tsks.

"It's not for you," he says.

"Why not?"

"Too hard."

"Maybe I like hard." I chug the booze, only then seeing Shodia pouring the alcohol down El'jah's throat. The drink, it seems, is not self-served. Others shoot it to you.

Red-faced, clearly trying to contain his cough this time, El'jah passes me his napkin.

The drink is pleasant. It goes down like water. What's the big deal? The second I think it, fire explodes in my belly and spreads over my lungs, threatening to spill out of my mouth like lava. I suck in a breath and start hacking into the napkin, an extremely unladylike behavior. The table roars with laughter while I'm bent over my knees with the wolf patting my back.

As the hacking calms and I train myself to breathe again, I overhear the males talking.

"You make quite the entrance, wolf."

"Lenox."

Lenox. A nice name. A name that triggers memories.

I wish memories didn't come, but they do. They come at the worst possible times, and they're pouring in now as I'm bent over, still trying to breathe.

The morning Marybell rushed into my chambers, startling me awake by grabbing my shoulders and shaking me, telling me the savages have entered the palace, and we must flee.

Me getting up and trying to exit via secret passages, but Father's males come into the rooms and take me.

I thought they were saving me.

I thought I was safe.

I was wrong. They took me into a room and ...

A deep male voice penetrates the memories. "You're okay," he says, and squeezes my hip, and that's when I realize I'm in a fetal position on the wolf's lap, and he's rocking me.

He tucks a lock of hair behind my ear. "What happened?"

I look around. People at the table are finishing their meals, and only the prince is staring right at me.

"I could ask you the same thing."

"You started shaking, then curled up and hugged me. And as much as I enjoyed that, I also smelled yer fear and disliked the cold sweat breaking out on yer skin, along with the trembling."

I cup my face. "I've made a fool of myself."

"No one saw," El'jah says.

"How come?" the lycan asks. He starts rubbing my back, making me feel better about today's disasters. I'm getting a headache, the same headache I had this morning. Glamour haze.

"I'm holding an illusion over the pair of you that will end...right about now." The prince snaps his fingers, and the headache disappears.

The wolf groans and shakes his head. "I've about had enough of this luncheon." His muscles tense. I think he means to stand.

I leap off his lap and sway on my unsteady feet. The wolf stabilizes me by grabbing my hip and elbow. "Easy now, lass. No rush."

El'jah stands with us. "I'll escort you back." He excuses himself from the table, and we stroll to the portal, where El'jah and I walk through. The lycan remains on the cliff.

"Did you forget something?" I ask.

"Lycans hate fae portal magic." El'jah says, amused. "Don't be afraid, puppy. We have cookies here in the sunny court. Come nibble on one." He pats my head.

The wolf grinds his teeth and steps through the portal, quickly moving past us, throwing a "Let's go" over his shoulder.

El'jah groans. "His mating scent makes me want to fuck the entire pack of 'em. And Gloriana?"

The lycan is now stopped, hands on his hips, waiting for me. We're in a private tower, not in the courtesans' tower, and that makes me nervous.

"Yes, Prince?" I address El'jah formally because of the tone of his voice and how he said my name. I grew up a princess. I know when a male in power is addressing me as his subject versus as his friend or acquaintance.

"You *will* tell the wolf about the miners hunting you."

I nod.

"You will tell him now."

"Goodbye, little prince," the lycan says.

El'jah leans in and whispers at my ear. "Bring your wolf to my very cozy party tonight."

"Yes, El'jah," I say at the same time as the wolf says, "No fucking way we're going to one of yer parties."

10

LENOX

After the prince leaves, the portal closes, and that tells me it's a gateway for private, not public, use. Nobody besides the royals and selected guards can pass through this area. The unfamiliar hallway with golden silk threads woven into thick royal-blue wallpaper gives an impression of opulence. My boots leaving dirt on red marble tiles with rich cursive carvings in the shape of leaves and budding flowers feels almost sacrilegious.

The fairies styled the hallway as if it's a divine reception area.

I crouch and run a claw over a single tile design, then stand and touch the golden silk thread on the wall. "Handmade." Incredible craftsmanship.

"Elven made," the princess says as she stands next to me. She points at the painting of a small castle at the top of a hill, which looks strangely familiar. "And that's mine."

I snap my head her way. "What do you mean yours?"

"I painted that." With a head tilt, she scrunches up her nose. "You can tell it's a child's work. I'm a much better painter now."

It occurs to me that I know absolutely nothing about my mate. She's a painter. A talented painter, one who manipulates oils over canvas and paints nature, an expression of art I appreciate. My people are one with the earth, the forest, the moon. We pray to Natra, our Mother Nature.

"How did the painting get here?" I ask.

A blush spreads over her cheeks. "I gifted it to the Summer king."

"Is that so?"

She blushes even more, then peeks up at me from under her bangs. "It was a long time ago."

Yeah, that does nothing to appease me. I cross my arms over my chest. "You had a childhood crush on the king?"

"Of course," she admits as if I asked something ridiculous. "Everyone crushes on the Summer king."

"Do they, now?"

She nods. "He's the Summer king. They call him the pussy magnet." She presses two fingers against her mouth. "Excuse my language."

"Yer language is excused, but you're not. I don't want to hear any more about the Summer king, and lass, once I've had you, I promise you won't remember what the king looks like. Let's go."

The Summer king is my competition. The Summer king! My life can't get worse. I finally mark my mate only to find out she's crushing on the king of the court where I'm staying.

I must leave said court.

Meanwhile, I plan on avoiding the king and shagging the king right out of my mate's memory. Mmhm.

I snatch her painting and tuck it under my armpit, then walk toward the guarded double doors. Paintings line the long hallway, and now I'm watching them like a damn hawk, trying to ascertain how many more paintings Gloriana has given him. At the door, the royal guards, dressed in black and gold, uncross their weapons.

Next to me, the princess looks up, probably confused about why we stopped.

"Any other paintings yours?" I ask before going into the room.

She shakes her head.

"Good." I barge inside and immediately get slapped by the scent of my mate's arousal. It is amplified because this is a fairy court with magic that invites coupling and enhances the senses. Mine are naturally heightened. I don't need any more encouragement. I'm only resisting mounting her by a thread.

Cursing, I lean my mate's art against the foot of a giant bed and touch the sheets. Not silk, but thick and rich cotton with a gray rabbit fur throw for decoration. The room colors are green, beige, and brown, natural and soft colors. The wood and leather decor is something one might find in a cabin in the woods. It makes me think the royals considered my culture as a source of inspiration.

The hospitality of the Summer fae is legendary. I appreciate the effort to make me feel "at home," though I still hate the Summer king for being so pretty. Arsehole.

On the left, before a curtained door leading to a terrace or a balcony, there's a burgundy love seat facing the bed. I take a seat and invite the princess inside.

"Come in," I tell her.

She's standing at the door, gaze on the bed.

"I won't fuck you right now. Come inside." This is a mating chamber. She is skittish, and I'm too old to understand her fear of my knob.

"Princess, don't fear my dick. It's only a knob, and I won't make you take it. Come in."

She's frozen.

"Gloriana," I say in the same tone I use when training wolf cubs. Finally, she looks at me. "Walk into the chamber."

She walks in, and the doors close behind her. The light bugs glowing on the walls ignite, providing soft light. The candles are lined up over the unused fireplace. Why does the Summer Court have a fireplace when their winters are marked by a cold breeze over the lands for only a few spans?

I approach the princess and lift her chin. Pretty hazel eyes look up at me. Her nose is perfectly straight, her lips lush, her skin tone darker than mine, her features identifying her as a descendant of the Stenan tribes. She is beautiful.

I glide two fingers over her cheek. Soft as a baby's bottom. A tint of fresh arousal enters my nose, and my cock jumps, lifting the kilt right off my knees.

"You are art itself," I tell her.

She gulps, appearing nervous, though not afraid. If she were afraid, I would smell it.

"This is the first time I'm alone with a female who is my mate," I say, trying to find something in common with her. I don't think I succeed, because she narrows her eyes.

"And what about those other times when they weren't your mate?"

"I don't recall them."

"Are you sure?"

This conversation went to shite fast. "Yeah, little lass, I'm sure."

A smile tugs her lips, and she blushes again. "Little lass."

I smile back, hoping I look sexy and not scary with my lips covering the edges of my canines. I picked that up from

Tolei the savage that one time we dined together. He kept his smile pleasant and hid his canines from his mate. "You like that I call you little lass?"

She nods.

I kiss her cheek and lift her into my arms, then carry her to the sofa, where I sit and put her on my lap. Her fragile arms encircle my neck, and she sits up straight on my thighs, her pretty face close to mine. She likes sitting with me like this too.

I close a hand over her throat, then slide my palm to the back of her neck and tug her forward so I can kiss her. Softly. Barely any touching of the lips. She tilts her head, her lips parting, seeking my tongue.

I wind my hand into her hair and open my mouth, letting her taste me while I fist her hair and grip her hip, grinding her arse on my cock. I swallow her little moans, and when she starts moving over my knob on her own, I arrange her so that she's straddling my lap.

Gloriana's face is flushed. Her submission sends shivers all over my body and makes my balls swell with seed.

I tuck the material she wears under her breasts and whisper, "At attention, ladies."

Large areolas shrink, and the nipples poke out like soldiers. I lick one, then blow on it, then do the same with the other, but this one I suck into my mouth, trying to fit the entire tit inside, my tongue under the nipple sucking like my pups are gonna suck it in the near future.

The princess throws her head back, and she rubs herself over my shaft, which is as hard as it gets. I want nothing more than to bend her over the bed and mount her like a bitch wolf, but I also enjoy watching her get herself off.

She's lost in her passion, her mouth open, her moans getting louder, rubbing herself over my cock more frantically. I grab her hips and help her with friction, watching her fuck herself on my covered knob.

It's dry humping.

She makes me feel young and less jaded. Perhaps I could live out some of her twenties in a way I couldn't live out mine.

I grew into an Alpha at a young age. While my peers sailed the seas, hopping from island to island, exploring forests, then returning home to settle with a female, I stayed in one place to make sure everyone had a home to return to.

I didn't have time for females to dry hump me.

I certainly didn't have a mate.

A wolf gets only one of those in his lifetime, so I better not fuck this up. (I'll fuck it up.)

The princess is near screaming. I press a hand over her mouth and one on her throat, squeezing a little to help her come. Sure enough, her body freezes, then starts quaking with an orgasm. "That's a good little lass. Come all over yer wolf's knob."

I release her throat and uncover her mouth, and she falls forward onto me.

Her tiny breaths tickle the side of my neck as I rub her back.

I hear her heartbeat.

Her mouth opens, her tongue sweeping her lower lip, and I want that little tongue sliding from my balls to the tip of my rod.

"What's a good little lass do after the wolf lets her use him?"

Gloriana lifts her head from my shoulder. "Whatever the wolf finds pleasing."

"On yer knees."

11

GLORIANA

The pulse of the lycan's toothmarks on the back of my neck matches the throbbing of my clit after I rubbed it all over the lycan's kilt, which is scrunched up under me, revealing a glimpse of his powerful, hairy thighs.

On yer knees, he said. I unfold from his lap and kneel between his legs, my breasts out, my skirt bunched around my middle.

"I like kilts," I blurt. I run both hands up his inner thighs, dragging the kilt up and up until I reach his cock. I fist it and realize the lycan is so big, I'll need to use both hands. And so I do.

I grab him with both hands and start pumping under the kilt.

He unsnaps it, and the material falls off so I can see his cock. It's massive, with a hard ring at the bottom. Semen leaks from the tip and provides moisture so my hands glide over the smooth skin.

The lycan spreads his legs further before leaning in and

stroking my face. "You've never done this before," he says. "Are you nervous?"

I nod, dreading even trying to suck him, because I don't want to do it wrong. I've never been good at much of anything besides painting and attracting powerful suitors at Father's palace. And I'm not even sure why I have to do it right for the lycan. It's not like I have to impress the wolf.

But I want to.

I want to hear *little lass* and *good lass* from him more than anything right now.

"There's nothing to be nervous about." He keeps stroking my cheek, his blue eyes at half-mast and glowing. I can tell he's turned on, and it encourages me to keep jerking him off.

"Put it in yer mouth and suck until yer cheeks are hollow and tears run down yer cheeks. Hm?"

I nod.

"Speak when I address you with yes or no. When I throat fuck you, tap out on my thigh when you've had enough. Clear?"

"Yes, wolf."

"Begin."

I lean in and put him in my mouth. The moment my tongue contacts his semen, I moan at the sweet taste of it. I lick and lick, groaning, and my body flares with heat, my belly churning, my breasts becoming heavier and heavier.

I pull back, gasping for air. "What is happening to me?"

"Yer body is recognizing her mate as a wolf female's body might."

"The fairies call it heat."

He nods. "That's right."

"But I'm a Stenan. We have no magic or heat."

He wipes his seed off the tip of his cock and runs his

thumb over my bottom lip. "You are a child of nature, a marked lycan mate, and yer body is preparing itself for when I mount you." He twists my nipple, and I lick the seed off the bottom of my lip, groaning at the sweetness.

I put his cock back into my mouth, eager for the drops of seed he feeds me as I suck. It makes me want to suck harder, until my cheeks are hollow and his cock is hitting the back of my throat, sometimes gagging me, forcing tears from my eyes.

The wolf kneads my breast with one hand. With the other, he twines his fingers into my hair.

He fists it and forces my head down so that his cock blocks my airway. He holds me there until tears stream down my cheeks.

I tap his thigh, and he lets go.

Gasping, I inhale before he forces his cock back into my mouth, gagging me again.

"You're doing a great job pleasing yer wolf, lass." His seed drips down my throat, and I'm so hungry for it, I don't tap out this time around, even when I should.

The wolf tilts his head before jerking me off his cock. I gasp a breath, while he leans in and whispers, "Tap out when you've had enough, is what I said. If I must teach you a lesson in obedience, I will. I dislike disciplining females, but if you want to be a little brat, I will discipline you gladly. You will not enjoy it."

"I'm sorry, wolf." I didn't mean to displease him.

"Thank you." He kisses my cheek. "You look lovely when you're flushed and eating my seed. Do you want to suck for more?"

I nod vehemently.

The wolf narrows his eyes.

He asked me to speak, not nod.

"Yes, wolf."

"Finish me off, then." He leans back, and I keep my eyes locked on his as I suck him in earnest, wanting a full stream of his seed.

I don't want him to scold me again.

I want to please him, get him off, so I suck him so hard, my jaw starts to hurt. Yet I don't stop. I don't stop because the wolf throws back his head and closes his eyes, his chest heaving. His claws scrape the wooden chair arms, and his body tenses just before his cock starts pumping seed into my mouth. The jet of cum is so forceful, I nearly choke on it.

Eagerly, I gulp it up, and when some of it spills past the corners of my mouth, the wolf wipes it away with his thumb and brings it to his mouth for a taste. *Oh boy.*

His cock stops pumping, and I let go of it. It falls heavily on his thigh, some seed still leaking out of the hole and trailing down the tip.

Eyes on the wolf, I stick out my tongue and lick.

He hisses, jaw tightening. "Crawl to the other side of the bed and grab a blanket between yer teeth, then crawl back and curl up on my lap."

My knees scrape the wood as I crawl on all fours, then bite the soft pink blanket and carry it between my teeth back to the wolf. Cheeks flaming, my body on fire from both arousal and embarrassment, I feel sexy while crawling, I do it with eagerness because it's going to earn me the *good lass* praise the wolf gives me.

I settle back between his legs.

He holds the blanket while I curl up on his warm lap. I lay my head on his shoulder, where I get to bury my nose in the crook of his neck and inhale the hearty scent of a strong male. He wraps the blanket around me along with his arms and sighs as if content to have me there.

My mother wasn't particularly affectionate.

Father even less so.

Maids and governesses raised me.

Rarely ever has anyone held me or ever hugged me. This is really nice, and I had no idea I needed this. Tears sting my eyes. I try not to cry and ruin this moment.

"You did well, little lass."

"Thank you, wolf." My chin quivers.

"My family calls me Lenox."

When I don't reply, he asks, "Did you hear me?"

"Yes." A tear slips out and lands on his shoulder.

"Yes what?"

"Yes, Lenox."

He kisses the top of my head. "Good lass."

He considers me his family. I guess a wolf would consider his mate family, but it's different for me, though not necessarily a bad thing to be part of a wolf's family. It's just that I also want freedom to explore what pleases me, and when I'm with the wolf, I want only to please him. Is that still doing whatever pleases me?

Gah, my brain is overthinking.

"Will you introduce me to your family?"

He nods. "You will like my sister Mackenzie."

"I'm sure I will." I sure hope so. Expecting he'll list more family members, I wait, but Lenox seems to have finished. I curl his hair around my finger.

Before he asks about my family, I change the subject. "Sometimes, back in Lyan, I would sneak out of the palace with Marybell, wearing maid's clothes."

"Oh yeah?"

"Mmhm. We would stroll the streets, and I would marvel at the freedom of those females coming and going from shops and diners and homes."

Under me, the wolf tenses. I continue. "Most times, I would return to the palace wishing I were one of those females."

"Why?"

"Because of the freedom their position allowed them."

"You mean they were not princesses?"

I nod, then correct myself. "Yes."

"I thought every lass wanted to be a princess."

"Until they are."

He lifts my chin. "What's wrong with being a princess?"

The wolf's blue eyes stare down at me with interest. He really wants to know. He's not simply making polite conversation, but instead, he's actually interested in what I have to say about growing up as a royal.

In fact, I think the wolf is interested in what I have to say in general.

He's interested in me, and that makes two of us. I'm interested in who I am as well.

"The princess has no voice of her own. Everything she does has already been decided for her, sometimes even before birth. She lives in a luxurious cage until she's traded into another cage that's hopefully more luxurious than the one of her birth, for that is all she will ever have. A cage with her things. I have many things. After the savages seized the country and raided the palace, they gave me my things back. But things mean nothing if I have no freedom."

"What is yer definition of freedom?"

"Attending a party. A real party where young people drink and talk and make out. Not a ball or a function, or a dinner. A real dirty-as-fuck party."

"Dirty as fuck?"

"Yes, Lenox. What do you say?"

He stares at me.

He's going to reject my idea, and we will argue, and I dislike arguing. "I want to get to know who I am with no things, no prospects, no marriages, no external pressures of any sort, and I want to do what other people my age do. Careless partying until the sun comes up."

The wolf scrubs his jaw.

I sit up more and curl my toes on his thigh. "The Summer king wouldn't invite me for a mating season. He kept me at the estate."

"I approve."

"I thought you might. I presume you docked on his shores, and he invited me to court on false pretenses, which I don't appreciate, but I can work with that now that I'm getting to know you."

"I'm relieved," he deadpans.

"The Summer Court in mating season is something to be experienced, and I would like to experience it in full swing."

"And you will experience mating, I assure you."

"No doubt, but I also want to attend parties, one such party tonight with El'jah. It's private and it sounded secretive, and I have to go."

The wolf tenses, his jaw working. "You don't have to. You want to."

"It feels like I *must* attend the party."

Lenox shakes his head. "The prince's parties are not for you."

"What do you mean?"

"I mean what I said. Not for you."

"How so?"

"They're sex parties, Gloriana."

"How do you know?"

The wolf snorts. "I ken."

"You've been to one." When he says nothing, I ask, "Have you?"

"I'm an old Alpha male werewolf."

Fine! I leave the comfort of his lap and stand. I fix my clothes. "I'm an almost-nineteen-year-old virgin princess with a wolf who wants to claim her. You'd better take me to that party, lycan, or I won't let you near my pussy." I square my shoulders.

The wolf's jaw loosens.

I think I shocked him.

Good. I am my father's daughter. I grew up in court. Dealing with powerful males was my life, and I am dealing with one here. I will be dealing with him for the rest of my life, it seems. It's important that he understands he can't walk all over me, even if I am his to claim.

"Marybell should be coming in with dress fittings," I say.

He chuckles. "Are you dismissing me?"

"I'd like to look pretty for you at the party tonight."

The wolf laughs as he stands and makes his way out, then stops at the door. He knocks twice, and the guards open it. Marybell stands there, and has likely been standing there for a while now.

Her eyes twinkle, and I blush profusely.

Lenox turns and walks backward down the hallway. "I'll pick you up at midnight."

I thrust my arms up in the air. "Woohoo!"

12

LENOX

My mate wanting to go to a sex party is not a problem.

My mate wanting to go to a sex party before I consummate the claim is the problem, and I cannot shag her yet for several reasons. One of them is that I'm on foreign soil where I can't control...everything.

I'm in a fae court with not a single wolf directly under my command. Rohan has been a rogue with his own male pirates since Freya married his brother. Over two decades, I reckon. The lack of complete control makes my wolf itchy and irritable, and I'm constantly on guard. The vigilance is taking a toll on me, and I have a feeling the leash I hold over my temper is the first that'll slip.

Maybe I'll take a bite out of the Summer king.

Happy thoughts.

Since I don't use fae portals, it takes me a long time to make my way back to the ship. In the belly of it, I gather my things into my old black leather sack, which has seen better spans, and shoulder it before leaving my quarters for the upper deck. There, I find Rohan, sitting between four nude fairies. Not two, but four. They're sunbathing.

The scene reminds me of why I hate that I promised to take Gloriana to the party.

But if I forbade the event, I'd be forbidding her personal freedoms, something that she is trying to explore. She would refuse me access to her body, and while I think it's cute she's threatening me with the power of her pussy, I also find it admirable. I didn't think she had it in her to stand up for herself.

AT THE BAR, I sit down with my back to Rohan and pour two shooters.

The fairies start moaning loudly, likely because they're touching each other.

My princess is going nowhere. I might buy a cage and carve her name on it. Another happy thought. Hmm. I bet Rohan has a cage somewhere that I could borrow.

I drink the whiskey. Or is it bourbon? It's nasty and cheap and burns its way down my throat.

I'll have another.

Rohan straddles the chair next to me and picks up his shooter.

Silently, we click the glasses together and drink.

"You smell like you emptied a sac into your hand and used your cum to style your hair." He sniffs my hair. "Eww."

The princess ran her hands through my hair after she finished me off.

I roll my eyes. Sometimes, I curse our keen senses. We can smell everything, but within the clan, it's something we don't bring up in conversation. While he'll always be a part of the clan, he's an outcast, sometimes by his choice, other times by my design.

During a major conflict, I stood by his brother and did what I thought was best for the clan at the time. I regret hurting Rohan, but he's a good male and forgives easily. When I asked him to bring me here as a personal favor, he didn't hesitate.

"I've missed you," I tell him.

When he doesn't respond, I glance over and find him looking far into the horizon.

"How is she?" he asks.

Freya. The love of his life and wife to his brother.

"She is well. As well as one can be after one loses a husband."

Rohan whips his head around. "What?"

"What what?"

"Lose a husband?"

Fuck. "I thought you knew."

"Knew what?"

I serve us two more drinks. "Yer brother passed away of lycanotrophia two winters ago. I'm sorry, Rohan." Lycanotrophia is a disease that causes the body to stop producing the fluids required to lubricate the joints so that we can shift into our animals. A lycan shifting back and forth from animal to male is as natural as breathing. One cannot live without breathing.

When we can't shift, we can go mad, or in the case of lycanotrophia, we can still shift, it's just painful and can cause the tearing of muscle and the breaking of bone.

Clearly in shock, Rohan blinks, then snatches the bottle from me and chugs the liquor down. He slams it on the bar and wipes his mouth. "Did you put him out of his misery?"

"I offered."

How can he not fucking know? It's been almost three turns. I drop a hand on his shoulder and pull him in for comfort. It's what an Alpha does for a clan mate.

"Freya put him down?"

"Mmhm."

"How could you let her do that?"

"I didn't let her. She..." I scrub my face, not wanting to have this conversation with Rohan right now, right here.

"Tell me!" he roars.

The four fairies he left behind scramble off the deck and leave the ship altogether. Rohan's males shout back, asking him if he's okay, and he replies he's fine, but he's so far from fine, he'll never be the same after I tell him what happened.

But I do tell him.

After all is said and done, we drink and talk about old times, celebrating his brother's life. During all this, I can't stop thinking about Gloriana and how there's no way I would leave Rohan right now for a stupid party she wants to attend. And yet it's not a stupid party for her.

I could tell it means something to her. Freedom, or whatever the fuck she thinks that means.

Damn it. Didn't even take me a span to mess things up between us. I said I would pick her up, and now I can't.

13

GLORIANA

The moon past the midnight position tells me Lenox is late. I'm pacing the mating chamber, wondering if he has an excuse or if I'm the gullible idiot who believed him. Moreover, he doesn't strike me as a male who's often late, so I also worry about him.

Not that I should care.

He bit me and said he wanted to claim me in a primal way, and I had to argue about attending something as minor as a party. After arguing for my freedom, and him agreeing to escort me, he's late anyway.

For the hundredth time, I pass the mirror, stop, and reassess my outfit.

I wore another outfit from the trunk he gave me back in Lyan. Not that he complimented or even noticed the first set of clothes I wore to the gathering. For a male who talks a lot about the mating love business, he sure seems to overlook the simple things, such as complimenting a lady on her looks or even acknowledging she's wearing something he gave her.

Gah! I sit on the sofa and bitterly cross my arms over my chest.

I spent an entire afternoon getting ready.

The Summer princess came and offered me her makeup and hairstylists. I wanted to look nice among the throngs of fairy females, which is no small feat to accomplish. I was sure Lenox would show up.

Naive, stupid Gloriana. He's over a hundred turns old, and he's manipulating you the way Father manipulated you and the way the king and prince of the Summer Court are manipulating you.

Males. All the same wretched creatures.

Which is why I should attend the party alone.

Standing, I square my shoulders and head for the doors, but just then, they swing open, revealing a pair of lycans all the way at the other end of the long hallway. Lenox walks in with his friend, acting as his friend's walking aid, because clearly, the other male is drunk and can't stand, let alone walk.

The male's hollering.

I'm sure he believes he's singing while holding up a bottle of something dark and powerful looking, maybe even dragon's fire itself.

"Princess," Lenox says by way of greeting. He strides right past me into the chamber, and, as if he owns the room, he deposits his drunken buddy on the bed. The male's arm falls over the edge of the mattress, and he drops the bottle.

I gasp.

Lenox catches the bottle before it hits the floor.

Impressive reflexes.

Cracking his neck, he sets the bottle on the nightstand, then stretches his arm over his head. There are claw marks under his armpit.

"Oh no." I look around for a clean cloth and spot one by the used bath that Marybell hasn't cleaned out yet. Where is she? I bathed a while ago. Hmm. I wet a white cloth and approach the lycan. Marybell's voice enters the chambers.

"I've got it!" Marybell is down the hallway, carrying a sack over her shoulder. She makes it to the room and drops the sack on the marble floor. It hits it hard and makes clinking noises, as if there're chains in there.

Next, she slings off an ancient-looking black leather backpack, then drags her feet to the sofa, where she collapses and throws her head back. She spreads her legs and arms and says, "Fuck it."

I glance at Lenox and catch him staring at me.

"What's going on?" I ask.

"Long story. Got a party to go to and no time to explain." He points at his wound. "Help me clean up."

"Coming, coming," Marybell says, and slogs over to the bath. She takes the cloth from my hand and proceeds to wash the lycan, careful not to aggravate his open wounds.

Marybell is my lady-in-waiting and my friend, my only confidante. She also knows how to treat wounded soldiers and is extending her services to the lycan in my room.

I hate it.

I hate that she's touching him, even with a cloth.

But I say nothing and stand there as she goes about washing his upper body, preparing him for the party.

When Lenox unsnaps his kilt and reveals his torso, I'm ready to punch him. Punch them both.

I extend a hand for the cloth. "Thank you, Marybell. That will be all."

Marybell places the cloth in my palm, curtsies, and leaves the chambers.

I throw the cloth at his head.

Lenox catches it and lazily starts washing his middle. "I was wondering when you were gonna make her stop."

"Oh, really?"

"She's yer lady."

"That's your body she's touching."

"My body is yours, lass, as yer body is mine, and if anyone so much as touches you with a pinky of his, I'll bite his entire arm off." Lenox walks past me and bends to grab the leather sack, leaving me with a full, albeit brief, view of his large ball sac dangling between his legs.

From the bag on the floor, he takes out a long black leather kilt and dresses, then changes his boots. He grabs oils and dabs them on his chest and the back of his neck. After tossing the oil bottle back into the bag, he rummages around and finds a brush for his hair. Once dressed and groomed, he moves on to the large bag.

From this bag, he pulls out long thick chains.

"We'll be leaving in a moment."

"Yeah, okay, take your time." What in the holy name is the male doing?

I take a seat on the sofa as Lenox chains the lycan to the only bed in our mating chamber.

The male is now snoring, none the wiser.

As if that's not at all odd, Lenox asks, "You ready?"

Standing, I pat my tiny dress, making sure it's covering my bottom. It does, barely, but that's the point of the outfit he gave me. "I am dressed." My heart is pounding in my ears. I'm fishing for compliments, and I can't seem to get any, because Lenox points to the leather bag.

"Pick out a leash for yourself. I have three."

"Hm?"

"The leash, lass. Pick one out."

Maybe he's crazy, and I'm now meeting the crazy side of him. Let's find out.

I peer inside the bag to find three leather leashes in white, brown, and black. I pick out the black one since it matches his kilt.

He stretches out his hand, and I drape it over his palm.

Lenox grabs my wrist and pulls out a thick black leather wristband from his kilt. He snaps it closed over my wrist, then hooks one end of the leash around the small metal loop on it.

There it is. The crazy. "What are you doing?"

He tilts his head. "Did you think I would let you run around loose at a private sex party hosted by the Summer prince?"

I nod. "Yes, yes, I did."

"Then you're confused, or I've been unclear about how my courting will proceed." He grabs my hip and pulls me to his body. "Which part of my courting was unclear?"

The oil he applied, sandalwood and vanilla, is heavy and musky and makes me want to lick it off him. It drowns his natural scent, and I wonder why he chose to do that.

He thinks this is courting. Oh boy. "How does a wolf go about courting?"

The wolf rubs his cheek against mine and tugs my leash. "Gently. He takes great care the princess enjoys it while he tries hard not to *unlive* anyone else in the process. Shall we?"

14

GLORIANA

The venue for the party is a guarded secret, and as Fleur explained, only a select audience gets an invitation. Her brother must've sensed something from the lycan male, Fleur had said, a desire of some sort that the prince can accommodate with the party.

I have no idea what the princess meant by "a desire of some sort," and I didn't even know how to get to the party. Not that I needed to, because around the Summer Court, the fairies have ways of directing people where they need them to go.

When Lenox and I walk out of the chambers, four, instead of two, guards stand in the hallway. At first, I think it's a shift change. It's not. The pair that have been stationed at the chambers all span long escort us toward a portal.

"Can we go on foot?" the lycan asks.

One of the guards shakes his head. "You're going to the prince's private island."

The lycan growls. "Never heard of it."

"That's because it's private," the guard says drily.

I chuckle, then clamp my mouth shut.

Lenox glares at me. "Something funny?"

"No."

"Didn't think so." He scowls at the portal, then at me, then back at the portal.

He's having second thoughts. I just know it.

"The prince guarantees your safety, as does the king," I say. "They would not want to ruin the mating season with an unexplained disappearance or any sort of event that could potentially hurt business for the summer."

The lycan shakes his head. "You trust the fairies. You shouldn't."

"She's right. We—"

The lycan's deep growl cuts off the guard who spoke and makes me step back. I never want to hear this sound again. It's terrifying, the sound of a massive animal ready to pounce.

"You think I'm being ridiculous about not wanting to go through portals," he says. "You wouldn't think that if you knew how the fae used the portals during their wars."

The guards exchange glances.

Lenox steps toward one of them. "The lycans never forget." He tugs my leash, and we step through the purple portal without the guards.

Immediately, I know we've made the right decision by coming here. We stand on a massive tree trunk that's rising out of the blue sea. Pixies float on top of leaves, playing stringed instruments, the music sexy and enticing. Bare-chested sirens with fluorescent pink and green and even blue hair the length of their bodies swim under the leaves, their fins flaring out in an elaborate show of vibrant color.

Ahead, near the shore, a small group of fairies lounge in the water, the soft waves washing over them. Some are nude, others barely clothed. They're chatting with merfolk perched on the shore, whose soft laughter sends electrifying sparks down to my clit. Some of those are mermales.

"I didn't bring a fan," I say.

"I doubt it would help."

He's right. It wouldn't, and I know it wouldn't because as my gaze travels farther up the shore, beyond the blazing fire in the pit, I see the fairy prince. He's standing with his legs spread and his head thrown back, his hands fisting the mane of a male kneeling before him.

When I realize what's happening, I gasp. Loudly.

The fairies look up, and the merfolk turn at my reaction.

I touch my fingers to my mouth.

Lenox threads his fingers through mine. "You wanted to come, remember?"

"And now I want to stay."

"Are you sure?"

I nod.

"Speak up, Gloriana."

"Yes, Lenox, I want to stay, and I want to lose my virginity to you on this perfect island on this perfect night."

One corner of his mouth turns up. "I took yer virginity last night."

He's toying with me. "Liar. You made me think we had sex when we both know I passed out. Come to think of it, where did you spend the night?"

A siren rises from the water and props her elbows on the tree trunk, making cleavage between her large breasts. The wrinkles around her eyes and mouth make me think she's an older siren. I didn't think they aged at all. The only ones I've ever seen were all young and flawlessly beautiful like the fairies.

She opens her mouth and speaks, but I can't hear anything.

The lycan crouches and touches her face, and she leans into his touch, her nostrils flaring, her sharp predatory teeth making me flinch.

In his native lycan tongue, Lenox speaks softly, and when the siren whines and sinks back under the sea, I know he refused her proposition.

Standing back up, he pinches the bridge of his nose.

"What's wrong?" I ask.

"The mental pressure to refuse a siren call has a price."

"Oh."

He blinks, and I note that the blood vessels in his left eye have burst. "We need to get ashore."

"How?" I ask.

"We swim." He tugs at my hand. "Ready?"

"I'm not a very good swimmer."

A mermale rises from the water. He has chin-length curly dark hair and eyes clearer than the cerulean seas. His shoulders are wide, his tattoos are sexy, his muscles incredible. "I can take you to the shore, milady."

The moment he proposes it, my belly flares with need, my breasts suddenly grow heavy, and my vision starts to blur out everything besides the mermale, who stares at me intently.

"Fight it," Lenox says.

I dip my toe into the water.

Lenox tugs my hand back. "Tell him you appreciate the offer and kindly decline."

I want to go with the mermale, but I also *don't* want to go with him. My head is starting to hurt.

A whistle sounds, and next to me, Lenox shouts, "Oh, little prince, yer subjects are propositioning my mate. You can rein them in, or I will eat fish for dinner."

The mermale sneers. I shake my head as Lenox growls

again, the sound that of a wolf warning of an imminent attack if the other male doesn't back off.

From the shore, the prince whistles, and the mermale sinks underwater, leaving us alone at last.

The spell breaks, and my headache subsides.

"You still want to stay?" Lenox asks.

"Yes."

"You're a persistent little thing, I'll give you that. Come on." He sits with his legs in the water and winds my arms around his neck so that my belly touches his back, then he sinks into the sea and swims. Under me, his powerful muscles shift, the oils he used on his body washing off and revealing an even more potent male scent.

I stick out my tongue and give his skin a lick.

Salty and male.

Oooo. I like it.

I lick again.

We reach the shore, and as if I weigh nothing, Lenox rises with me on his back. I hang off his neck, not wanting to let go. He pries my hands off, then reaches back to grab my hip with one hand and moves me to stand in front of him. Without warning, he slams his mouth on mine and practically starts invading my mouth.

I grab his shoulders and dig my fingernails into his skin, one leg coming up and over his hip. He catches it under my thigh and lifts me while he starts walking. We make out until my back hits something rough.

Lenox lifts our leash-connected hands and pulls back. I look up above my head and see the leash is looped around a branch and I'm pressed against the trunk, one leg over the lycan's hip, my pussy exposed.

Inside my body is an inferno. "Take me now."

"No."

"You want to." I can feel how hard he is and see how he's looking at me. He wants me, and I want him.

"Not now," he bites out.

A whine escapes me. I rub my core against his hardness the way I did earlier on the sofa. I'm so hot and horny, I must get off.

Lenox moves his jaw against my cheek as a wolf might brush his muzzle against my hand when asking me to pet him. "Calm down, little lass, and inhale the scent of yer wolf."

I bury my nose into the crook of his neck and inhale so loudly, I snort. Something trickles down my thigh, and Lenox swipes it with his finger. A moment later, he's pushing the finger into my mouth, and I taste myself.

"The fairies have made a puddle of lust out of you. I consider it both a gift and a temptation."

"I want to hang out with you, wolf."

"And you will." Lenox pushes off my body, his blue eyes ablaze with lust. He blinks and scrubs his face, speaking his native tongue in a way that sounds suspiciously like cursing.

"You must learn a lesson, sweet little princess," El'jah says as he walks up to us. He is wearing a loincloth over his middle and is glistening from a slick of oils on his body. "And the lesson is that you need the lycan to survive the Summer Court and beyond. Come now, let's eat and drink."

Lenox releases me from the tree. We walk to the group of people gathered on the shore and sit with them. Lenox sits behind me, and I lean against his body. He's warm and safe, and while I don't know anyone in the group, I strike up conversations easily.

As the night goes on, I meet everyone and everyone meets me. While I've always loved social events, I also always watched my tongue and my demeanor, careful not to be too eager, nor too timid when it comes to conversations. But now that I'm not a princess anymore, I conclude I'm quite outgoing and have lots to say.

For the first time in my life, I feel like I can be myself and get an odd sense of belonging that comforts me. I don't know if I belong among these fae gathered in the quiet, small party on the shores or if it's that I feel I belong with the lycan, who says very little the entire night. He's a quiet, steady presence at my back who lets me be me.

The sun is rising, and the party retreats into the cabins hidden among the palm trees.

The prince waves at us before retiring for the span. It occurs to me that he's not staying while everyone he brought here is.

Once everyone disperses, Lenox and I remain sitting on the sand, waves gently washing over us.

"Did you have fun?" he asks.

I nod. "Did you?"

When he doesn't answer, I turn and catch the glow of his eyes.

"What matters to me is that you did," he says.

"That's strange."

He frowns. "What's strange?"

"That it matters I liked something. It never mattered before."

"Before you mated a wolf, you mean."

I nod. "No male has spoken to me the way you do." Nobody's ever cared if I had fun. Nobody's ever cared about me at all, I realize. Not just males either. Even my own mother used me to preserve her position for as long as possible.

I yawn and cover it with the back of my hand.

Lenox stands and wipes his palms together to brush off the sand. "Let's get you to bed."

I point behind him. "There's an open portal behind you."

Lenox tenses and turns slowly, his claws flexing. I stand beside him. On the other side of the portal is a misty evergreen forest. I look from the lycan to the portal.

"Do you recognize the place?" I ask.

"Aye. It's my forest."

"How can you tell?"

"I pissed on most of the trees there, creating my territorial boundary."

"Ah." Duh. He's a wolf. "To me, trees are trees, and I can't tell one forest from another."

We don't speak for a long time. The prince opened a portal for Lenox to head home. I don't know why El'jah would do such a thing, but I imagine it was because he had a knack for knowing the lycan desires to go home. Anyone willing to notice could see how uncomfortable and out of place Lenox is in the Summer Court.

Even at this small party tonight. He was quiet, barely said a word all night.

"Come home with me," he says.

Oh my... What now?

15

LENOX

The prince of the Summer fae offered me a direct passage home. In a few steps, I could be in Eleanor's Forest, which stretches across my clan's land. And I am certain it's my forest and none other, even though "trees are trees" to my mate.

I know these trees and this passage between them where the trunks, much like the one the fairies used to get us onto this island, rise from the forest ground. The fae used this portal during their wars, when they invaded our lands and massacred my people.

Times have changed indeed.

I drank and partied with fairies.

Luckily for me, my mate isn't a fairy, or I'd have a problem securing her safety against some of my own clan members, the ones whose hatred for the fae was passed on from father to son, mother to daughter.

Bringing a Kilseleian princess into a clan of lycans will create some issues, but she's not a threat. She's an innocent lass, and knowing she'll be surrounded by hundreds of males sends my protective instincts into overdrive. It also makes me want to grab her and run through the forest to get home as quickly as possible so I can lay her on my bed and claim her. Over and over again.

I asked Gloriana to come home with me, and she's not answering me. "What the fuck is there to think about?"

"I would leave everyone I know to go to a strange place where I know nobody."

"You only really know Marybell, and I will send for her when I take care of Rohan. Besides, you didn't have any problems making friends with unfamiliar fae tonight, so you should have even fewer concerns with my people."

"Oh yeah?"

"Mmhm. We throw better parties."

She smiles, her eyes struggling to stay open from tiredness. "The Summer Court is famed throughout the world for its parties."

"That's only because the world hasn't been invited to any of ours."

"Because you piss on the trees and it's keeping the world away?"

I laugh. She's funny, my lass. "That's right."

She laughs with me, then bites her lip, gaze on the portal. "I don't know, Lenox. I have no clothes, nothing."

"You have until I count to three to say yes."

"What?"

"One." I lift a finger. She stares, eyes wide and awake now. "Two. I will pick you up and run."

"What if my answer is no?"

"Not an option. Three." I sweep her off her feet and throw her over my shoulder and jump into the portal. On the other side, my body shudders, and I turn to see the portal still open behind me. I'll send someone for it. Right now, magic courses through my body, and I begin to transition into a werewolf. I twist and arrange my mate over my back as I did when we swam.

"Hang on. I'm taking you for a run."

The moon shines through the branches. I turn my face up toward it and close my eyes. Magic ignites the change in my body from a male to a werewolf, a warrior form that is both a male and a wolf.

"Don't be afraid," I tell my mate, my voice mangled as I speak with my longer than normal tongue and much larger teeth.

"I'm not," she whispers at my ear.

It takes everything I have not to throw her onto the ground and mount her the way I'd mount a female in heat. Gloriana's heat is different since she is of Stenan origins, but I can smell it and sense it because she's mine.

Her small hands run through the fur at the top of my shoulders. "It's coarse."

She sounds disappointed. I give her my profile, seeing her from the corner of my eye. "What did you expect?"

"Maybe something softer."

"When we have pups, their fur will be softer. Until then, you get what you get." Softer. Pfft.

I crouch and hold her wrists tightly around my neck before leaping and then running between the trees. Gloriana screams herself hoarse at first, then accepts her fate as I start climbing the mountain to reach the clan's main settlement, which we call the Mar's Den or just the Den.

The lycans on patrol in the forest hear me running and howl.

I don't greet them back. I want to return as quietly as possible. I'm not ready to deal with the clan yet. I cannot. I must consummate the claim before I can introduce her to my clan. An unconsummated mating claim makes my wolf agitated and snarly, and the foul mood of the Alpha male spreads through the pack like a disease.

My job is not to infect my clan with a bad mood.

My job is to protect my clan and make it stronger by breeding more Alpha males. Or Alpha females, if the divine nature is inclined. We have not been blessed with a female Alpha pup in over half a century.

There's a slight time difference between here and the Summer Court, and it affords me an opportunity to slip into the den from the secret forest passage I dug for my baby sister so she could escape the slaughter if I lost to my uncle, Rohan's father.

I won the bloody fight.

The rebellion afterward.

Now the clan is mine.

And I'm bringing my mate, not a wife or a female I wanted to breed. An actual mate formed by a rare and precious bond between two people. Since we haven't had a mated pair in over fifty turns, I believe Natra will now let us mate with other creatures, and while mating a Stenan creature might offend another lycan, I relish my mating claim to the Stenan female.

Making sure nobody is watching, and before the wolves on patrol catch up to me, I find the lever disguised as a mushroom and pull. The passage in the ground opens, and I descend the few steps, closing the passage door behind me.

It's a dark tunnel.

I need no light to see, but Gloriana does. "Don't be afraid, all right?" I walk. No need for running now. I await her answer, and when she doesn't give me one, I tap her wrists around my neck. "Answer me." I dislike disobedience and miscommunication, which is why I require everyone in the clan to speak their mind clearly. I want to hear her say *yes, wolf* or better yet *yes, Alpha.*

Gloriana shrugs and tends to roll her eyes, wave her hands, shuffle her feet, nod, and exhibit all manner of body language she thinks I understand. But for me, body language should support, not replace, verbal communication.

I listen to her breathing. It's calm and heavy. I hold her by the arse so she won't fall off my back while I move her around my torso and into my arms.

Her head rests on my biceps as I hold her the way I'll hold our pup someday. Her lips are slightly parted, and she is sleeping.

She's sleeping deeply.

Wow. I can't even.

"An Alpha male lycan put you on his back and ran up the mountain so he can lock you in his lair and breed you, and you slept through the trip?" I say, shaking my head. "But you don't even know where you are," I whisper hiss. "Yer instincts are...fuck all. You have none. Oh no..." I keep walking. "Oh no, lass, no. This will not do. We must work on yer instincts. If we don't, I will chain you to my body and won't separate from you, which will be great for me, but a loss of freedom for you. You understand?"

The lass in my arms continues sleeping.

A part of me, the part that's not worried about her well-being in the clan, is secretly thrilled that my mate trusts me and has given me complete control of her body, knowing I will take care of her.

16

GLORIANA

The miners will all die under the claws of the savage males that are advancing up the palace floors. I'm sitting in the corner, knees pulled up, terrified of what the three miners hovering over me will do. They're hungry for revenge, a sackful of flesh, as they call it.

They want me.

Before they die, they want to punish me for my father's sins.

A fourth miner marches into the room, and rips the tiara off my head, taking a handful of my hair with it. I scream as my scalp burns, and I cry because I'm afraid of what they'll do to me.

But they don't get to hurt me.

Growling comes from behind the fourth miner. All four of them start backing off, calling up their magic.

I'm too afraid to look at the creature that's growling. It's a medeisar, a creature that will devour us all.

The beast snarls, and I curl up into a ball and cover my head, close my eyes, and pray it finishes me quickly after it's done with the miners, who scream in agony as the creature tears them apart.

Calm arrives all too quickly, and it's my turn.

I hear the claws click over the stone as the creature approaches and sniffs around my arm. Terrified, I tremble.

When the creature doesn't attack, I dare to peek out from under the arm covering my head.

And meet his ice-blue eyes.

Gasping, I awake with a start and meet a pair of ice-blue eyes. I scream and push the male away, but manage to shove myself over the edge of the bed instead.

I fall right off, my ass hitting the wooden floor and bouncing twice before settling down.

I stay there, lying down, staring at the unfamiliar wooden ceiling.

This is not my bedroom in the palace.

Or my bedroom in the estate in the Summer Court.

Or the room in the courtesans' tower.

Or the mating chambers.

This is somewhere in the woods, judging by the design. Wooden floors, ceilings, and even a single worn-out wooden chair by the unlit fireplace, and a massive wooden bed with crisp white sheets that hang from it.

"Hello?" I call out.

Lenox pops up above me, a smirk on his handsome face, blue eyes twinkling. They're the same eyes I saw in my dream. That's not how this dream usually plays out. It always ends badly for me, except this one time. I have the wolf to thank for that.

"Hi," he says.

Oh, he's sexy. I mean he's really sexy, with sleepy blue eyes that are framed in charcoal as if someone lined the edges of his eyelids and painted his long dark lashes. His nose is large and masculine and straight, and his lips are plush. His jaw is square and hard.

A strand of dark hair falls over his right eye, and I reach out and tuck it behind his ear.

"Good morning," I say.

Lenox rubs his mark on the back of my neck. It's both soothing and arousing. I rise to my knees and press my lips to his.

"Where are we?" I ask.

"In my chambers."

"And where are your chambers?"

"In the den."

"The wolf den?"

Nodding, he keeps stroking the mark and angles my head to the side so it exposes my neck. He trails his mouth over my skin. My body's awake and heating up, and I widen my legs, wanting him to touch me between the thighs. When he doesn't, I try to get back in bed with him.

"Remain on yer knees on the floor."

My channel pulses. This wolf says all the right things.

He throws a pillow down, and I frown, thinking he wants me to sleep. That can't be right.

"For yer knees," he explains.

Oh. Duh.

He throws another pillow on the floor. "For my knees."

His? Huh?

Lenox slings his feet over the bed and stands next to me. He's completely nude.

His body is a display of power in every muscle a male could have. He's built more like a Savage horde male than a fairy male, with broad shoulders, a tapered waist, and large, powerful thighs. He's big and tall and rather hairy.

Body hair is not fashionable where I come from, so many males and all the females have it removed at an early age. Most female fae are born without body hair at all, and that's what I'm used to seeing.

The dark hairs on his thighs make him somehow more masculine, if that's even possible.

I can't resist.

I run a palm up his thigh and through the coarse hairs.

Lenox groans as he stretches, his thigh muscles flexing before he crouches beside me and strokes my cheek. He pushes a thumb into my mouth while the other hand trails over my back, leaving goose bumps in its wake. He grabs my bottom and squeezes, a low growl developing at the back of his throat.

It's not a threatening deep growl I heard before, but a more alluring tone, almost as if he's purring. Except, wolves don't purr.

He smacks my bottom.

I gasp, and Lenox catches it with his mouth, pushing his tongue inside. I grab his shoulders, and he smacks my bottom again and groans as I yelp into his mouth.

Next, his thick fingers touch my entrance, and I nearly jump as if electrified. My pussy spasms, and the next thing I know, liquid leaks out of my opening.

Oh no. I hope he won't notice! Is this even normal?

Lenox pulls back, his eyes blazing blue orbs. "Oh, my sweet lass, you are setting to make a puddle of lust on my floor."

Embarrassed because my liquid is trailing down my left thigh, I clamp my knees together.

Lenox tsks and slaps my bottom. "Open."

When I part my knees again, wider this time, he smirks and traces his big finger over my entrance. Back and forth, back and forth. It feels so good that I close my eyes and move with it but the moment I do, Lenox grabs my throat and steadies me, not letting me move. He strokes me, my body unable to please itself, and I realize Lenox enjoys controlling my body.

He enjoys controlling everything.

"Bend over the bed," he says, then kneels behind me.

Before I move, his hands are on my hips and lifting me over the bed so my bottom half is exposed to him. He'll see the liquid now, and I am completely and thoroughly mortified so much that I bury my face in the sheets. When I inhale, it's a scent of forest and earth and evergreen.

The scent makes me want him more. I grip the sheets as Lenox spreads my ass cheeks and licks from my clit all the way to my small pucker hole, where he lingers and probes with his rough tongue.

I never thought anyone would ever think of licking that hole, and after the liquid trailed down my leg, I didn't think I could be any more embarrassed, but I am. Lenox is doing things to me I never thought possible. It occurs to me I haven't the slightest clue what I'm doing, while he's the expert at all things sex.

It's a good thing he likes control, because all I have to do is obey.

I can do that.

He squeezes my bottom again, and I brace for impact.

He lands several hits on my bottom and a few stings on the back of my thighs, then swipes a finger over my slit.

"You're leaking heat, Princess. Tsk tsk tsk."

Oh no, he's bringing up my shame. I gulp, but then remember he likes answers and for me to acknowledge that he spoke.

"Yes, wolf," I mutter.

"Why are you leaking heat?"

"Because..." I wet my lips, and he licks my pussy again,

groaning while sucking on my clit. Oh, it's nice. Feels so good. I push back against his mouth.

He removes his tongue. "Because?"

"Because I'm aroused."

His body folds over mine, and his fingers move the hair away from the back of my neck. I shiver even though Lenox is warm and large framed and it feels like the safest place in the world is where I am now. Right under him.

He kisses the marking, then says, "I will penetrate you. It will hurt."

I hold my breath as the tip of his cock touches my entrance and Lenox pushes inside my pussy.

"Breathe out," he says, and I do. He pushes inside more, then retreats. "Breathe in now." He stays out while I breathe in, and when I start exhaling, he's back inside me.

He kisses behind my ear. "You are such a good little lass for yer wolf." He's fucking me slowly, gently penetrating farther and farther, stretching me so that it's not as painful as I expected.

Actually, it's pleasant, and I'm starting to like it.

Lenox seems to sense the moment the pain turns into pleasure, because he picks up his pace and grabs my throat. "You're not allowed to move," he says. "Not this time, not when yer blood is fresh on my knob, and I'm crazy with wanting to fuck you into the bed." He squeezes my throat, restricting my breathing, and rises behind me while pinning me down and fucking me until I scream with orgasm.

17

LENOX

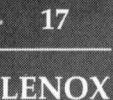

Under me, my little lass doesn't move while I empty inside her.

I don't move either, although I must before my knob end inflates inside her little pussy. She'll need a few more rounds on my cock before I can knob her up.

Tearing my mate's pussy, the same pussy that will give me so much pleasure during my life and birth me pups, is not on my agenda. It never will be.

Groaning, I withdraw from her, my knob slapping against my thigh. Gloriana's eyes widen, and she turns so red that I chuckle and kiss her cheek. "What is it?"

"Nothing."

The blushing virgin. Or ex-virgin. Either way, the princess is very cute and all mine.

I lean back on my heels and see liquid on the floor. "You made a puddle, lass." I tsk at her. "I'm tempted to make you clean it up with yer tongue."

Gloriana whips her head around. "You wouldn't."

Oh, I would, but she doesn't need to know that right now. I slap her bottom and climb onto the bed, then lean my head against the headboard. I tap my chest. "Come here."

She crawls over the bed, her breasts swaying, and the sight of her fucked and blushing makes me hard again. The princess's gaze drifts down to my stiffening cock, but she manages to meet my eyes and lay her head on my chest.

Finally, I am mated, feeling whole and at peace.

I sigh so loudly that I growl a little.

I am so happy.

I haven't been this happy and content since the morning I first spotted her. That vision, that moment in time when a wolf recognizes his mate, is one of the most magical moments in his life. The bliss after claiming my mate is akin to that moment. I am calm now, for she is here with me, where I can protect her and care for her and fuck her whenever I please.

Life is good.

Just one more thing.

"Gloriana," I say.

She lifts her head from my chest. "Yes?"

She's so pretty, especially now, with her eyes bright hazel and curious.

"Yes?" she asks again, because I'm staring at her beauty.

Right. What was I going to ask her? Ah yes. "Did you have a bad dream?"

Immediately, she tenses, and I know I'm on to something serious. Shaking her head, she says. "No, not a bad dream."

"You often wake up and fall off the bed?"

"No, wolf."

"Twice now, near early morning, you start moaning in yer sleep and clench yer fists as if you're fighting something." Or someone. The night I spent guarding her in the court, she moaned and clearly had nightmares.

She's looking everywhere other than at me. "This is really a nice bedroom." She points at the headboard. "Also very nice woodwork."

She's evading. I make the decision to let her do that this one time. "Thank you."

"Is it elven made?"

"Actually, I made it."

She blinks and looks from me to the headboard. "It looks elven. The handiwork is perfect, the patterns almost indistinguishable from one another. You're very good."

"My mother was part elf."

"Really?"

I nod, hoping she doesn't ask much about her. My mother was a clan whore. Nothing less, nothing more. I'd love to tell my mate elaborate sob stories of my upbringing, but luckily, my mother gave me up early on. My uncle taught me all there is to know about her, namely that she was a whore who enchanted my father and turned him against his clan.

"Did you want to see the rest of our corner?"

She frowns. "Our corner?"

I nod and sit up, letting her guide this conversation. I will hear about her fears sooner or later. I hope sooner so that I can protect her against the miners who are threatening her, but her fear of them is strong, and I don't want to force her to talk about them. At least not at this moment.

My lass is curious, and she ought to explore her new home now. I don't want her to meet the clan yet, but that's only because we're newly mated, and I want to put her in a cage and keep her next to my bed.

I tap her shoulder. "Corner, because my room is in the corner of the hall and secluded from the rest of the den. Do you want a tour?"

She rolls over and stands. Before I join her, I watch her walk to the window and part the blinds. Her perfect, long, slender legs carry her outside onto the terrace.

"Holy Ensna. This is where you grew up?"

I stroke myself a few times, then scratch my balls. She likes my land. "Aye. This is Eleanor, Lycana, the safest town in the world." Safest because I secured every miner I could find and brought them to my shores so that when Gloriana arrives, she will be able to identify the men.

Pfft. The fairy prince thought I didn't know about the threat on her life. I don't need a fairy to tell me of threats to my mate. Everyone is a threat, and I keep threats close, where I can control them.

"It's beautiful." Gloriana turns and smiles. "You coming?" With her back to the woods, she grabs the terrace rail and hops up on it, twining her feet around the iron railing below to secure her position.

I leap out of bed and sprint to the terrace, snatch her up, and practically throw her back on the bed.

Wide-eyed, she stares at me. "What did you see? What's wrong? Is it a dragon? I heard they fly over lycan villages and burn them to the ground."

"What? No, it's not a flying fire-spitting dragon. It's you!"

"Me?" She seems shocked.

I walk away and rest my palms on the wall, then hang my head. Calming down, I breathe slowly and deeply. "Princess, listen to me. You are the single most precious thing I care about, and you are not allowed to sit on the railing thousands of stones above the ground where you could fall to yer death."

When she doesn't answer, I glance in her direction.

Gloriana approaches me, then presses a hand on my

belly. My abdominal muscles contract, and my knob shoots semen on the wall. I want to fuck her again.

Like a seductive little siren, she ducks under my hand and appears before me so I'm caging her against the wall. One leg goes up and over my hip, and she thrusts her breasts toward my face. "Wolf, I understand your concern. It won't happen again."

I didn't expect this.

She strokes me, drawing out more cum.

I capture her wrists and trap her arms above her head. "Don't tempt me, lass."

"I want the knob end."

Fuck me. "Not yet." I kiss her mouth and slap her bottom. "Now we tour, meet the clan, and eat. Aren't you hungry?"

She starts lowering to her knees.

I grab her shoulders and keep her upright, and I cannot believe I'm doing it.

I have waited turns to claim my mate, and rejecting her attention outright feels like taking a hammer to my balls. But if she sucks me, I fear my control will slip. And I would hate that.

For one, I love controlling myself and others.

For two, if I lose control, I would tear her on the inside, and she's too tight for the knob end.

A pout forms on her mouth, and it's cute (and fuckable), and I want to nail her to the wall and pound into her mouth, pussy, arse...all her holes.

I love these happy thoughts. They soothe me.

Gloriana's belly growls. I raise an eyebrow. She is hungry after all.

"Saved by the growl." Taking her hand, I walk her to the wardrobe, only then realizing that the closet I made is far too small. I mated a princess who probably has ten carriages of clothing on their way here. What was I thinking when I made this thing?

It'll have to do for now.

I open the wardrobe and move aside so she can pick out some clothes, mostly soft cotton in lycan fashions. Comfortable and light, the clothes are also inexpensive so when we tear them either by accident or on purpose, we won't give a rat's ass. I don't know why I didn't secure a seamstress for her. Dresses. Gowns. A damn headkerchief, even.

"It's only until you can get your trunks from the court."

"And the estate."

Mmhm. I'll need to add a structure for the closet the way the fairies do. They've rooms upon rooms of closets, and in the court, her closet was in the area right beside her bedroom. I'll never understand the obsession with pieces of cloth, but I'm not going to begrudge my princess, and I certainly won't require her to dress like a lycan female. The last Kilseleian princess ought to keep any style she wishes.

The princess sifts through the racks, back and forth, back and forth. She picks out a black-and-white dress and holds it out for me to take. I'm not Marybell, but Gloriana is unconsciously expecting me to hold her garments. My sister, when picking out which dress to wear, hangs the clothes over the wardrobe door.

Not the princess. People hold her selections for her.

She picks out another and another and another.

I'm starting to feel less like an Alpha werewolf and more like a hanger for the four dresses my mate's trying to select. After she gives me the fifth dress, she closes the closet.

Finally. We will leave. Just have to drape one of these over her body, and be done with it.

Gloriana chews her bottom lip, picks up one dress,

makes a face, then hangs it back over my finger, only to pick up another dress, this one hanging from my middle finger.

No, she dislikes this one. She drops it back. The third and fourth dresses are no good either, and at this point, I've started praying the fifth one makes the cut, because if not, I think she might spend the rest of the morning selecting what to wear.

The fifth dress is a blood-red cotton dress that rises high midthigh, with a deep cleavage. The princess nods.

Who put this thing in there?

I shouldn't be surprised the princess picked out the most revealing one of the five. Even though she comes from a rather conservative Kilseleian court, staying at the Summer Court will change a person quickly, especially a young lady like Gloriana.

Therefore, my sister will never step her pretty wolf foot in a fae court. Nope. Never.

As if summoned, Mackenzie knocks on the chamber door. I know it's her because she knocks once, then pauses, then twice, then pauses, then three times.

"Brother," she whispers from the other side, "are you in there?"

Gloriana widens her eyes and hustles into the dress. "I'm not ready to meet your family." She straightens the dress and rushes to the window. There, she stands to the side, letting the light hit one side of her pretty face. She pulls back her shoulders, lifts her chin only slightly, and folds her hands in front of her.

She looks like she's posing for a portrait. Formal royal behavior will take some getting used to.

From the same closet, I grab the single item that is mine. A new kilt. Sage green for a change, and in a few moments, I'm dressed. "Come in."

Mackenzie storms inside the way she does everything, with the energy of one thousand suns. She bypasses me entirely, and when I think she might tackle Gloriana, she stops before her and gathers up her loose sweatpants as a lass might gather up her skirts.

She curtsies and stays low.

I snap my head up and stare at Gloriana, who's delighted at the formal greeting. At least at first. Many thoughts and emotions seem to pass through her mind, and her expressive hazel eyes reveal most of it, namely the initial happiness and familiarity, then sadness or perhaps nostalgia. I will find out which later.

When my sister remains down with her head bowed as is proper when greeting a princess of a Kilseleian or fae court, Gloriana says, "Oh, please rise. I'm not a princess anymore."

"Sure you are," I say.

Mackenzie stands, practically bouncing on her feet. She clasps her hands before her chest. "You're so young and pretty," she squeals. "And we're sisters!"

Gloriana smiles widely, showing all her teeth, and her eyes light up like the trees we decorate for the harvest moon.

"Come," Mackenzie says. She threads her arm through Gloriana's and pulls her toward the exit.

Gloriana stalls. "I need shoes."

"Whatever for?" Mackenzie keeps pulling the princess.

"Um..." Gloriana throws her head back and looks at me, but I say nothing because the shoes I got her are too small for her feet, and I'd rather she not see I misjudged her foot size. Lycans don't often wear shoes, so we have only one shoemaker in town. I'll need Gloriana to commission what she needs.

"Mackenzie," I call out after my sister who's already

down the hallway, passing one of my omega wolves who was on patrol.

"Do I get a hug or a greeting of any sort?" I shout after my sister.

"Later, bro!" She disappears around the corner.

The omega wolf greets me with a nod. "Alpha."

"Good morning, Alistair. What do you have for me?" I hoped I'd have a span of rest, but it doesn't seem like that's going to happen.

"The launa sent me to tell you welcome back."

I snort, knowing the Alpha female of the clan wouldn't send him only for that. "What is it?" Reluctantly I leave my chambers.

"We have a problem."

"We always do. What is it?" I repeat.

He gulps, but doesn't answer me right away. Hating to have to ask for something three times, I glare. "Answer me.'"

"She wants to hear about the princess."

18

GLORIANA

Lenox's sister is as short as the Summer fairy princess Fleur. But that's where the similarities end. Fleur's blonde-and-blue-eyed appearance reminds me of sunlight, while Mackenzie's dark eyes and raven hair pulled up in a messy ponytail remind me of twilight.

I find her pretty and friendly. When she smiles, showing dimples, it makes me smile too as she leads me down the long hallway, then takes a sharp left and exits. Bright light blinds me, and I shield my eyes, immediately noticing the temperature drop.

Goose bumps rise on my skin. I crinkle my eyes and peek between my fingers. The first color I see is green. I blink, letting my vision adjust, and open my mouth, popping the pressure in my ears.

This property, fenced in by tall evergreen trees, makes me feel like we're at the top of the mountain. Wolves of all shapes and sizes appear along the edges of the forest. Flashes of yellow magic sparkle as the wolves turn into males, making the forest come alive.

The people are making their way across the meadow, heading somewhere on my right, but I can't see where, for the wall next to me blocks the view. Mackenzie stands with her back to the forest. Her eyes are not those of a wolf. They're elven. Dark, wide, then tapering at the corners.

"Come on. Let's eat, and I'll show you around the den." She turns and marches across the meadow.

My bare feet land on coarse, rich grass that's definitely not an elven carpet. Pausing, I curl my toes. Seldom used to walking barefoot and rarely outside my chambers, I'm a bit out of sorts, though don't say anything, because Mackenzie isn't wearing shoes either. Besides, she's walking so quickly that if I don't hurry along, I might lose her in the crowd.

Or not.

It now occurs to me that every other person in the meadow is a male wolf. A nude male wolf.

It's getting crowded as I near a wide entrance that leads to a massive square structure that might be a fortress. Or what they call a den.

Mackenzie turns and sighs, then walks back and threads her fingers through mine again. She's practically dragging me. "Come on. I don't want to miss breakfast, and the night patrol got in ahead of us, which means they'll eat everything."

"Is that who these men are? Night patrol?"

Mackenzie stops and levels me with a stare. "There are no men here. Even our weakest omega is ten times stronger than a man."

"I apologize for the offense." It is a slip I learned from Father's court. Lycans are proud creatures, and strength is a measure of their worth. I know better. Damn it.

"We are males and females," Mackenzie says as we keep walking.

Once we're almost at the entrance, the wolves start turning, their noses wrinkling and lifting. A sea of blue eyes brightens like lanterns, and the males start growling low in their throats.

Mackenzie pauses, chewing her lip.

"What's wrong?" I grip her slender but firm biceps.

"They're smelling your heat, I think. Has my brother not claimed you yet?"

I'll never get accustomed to the ways wolves and fae discuss mating. Openly, without any reservations, as if it's the most natural thing in the world to chat about over tea. "He has." I clear my throat. "This morning."

"Only?" Her eyes widen.

I'm unsure how to respond to her surprise, so I smile politely, hoping she'll continue talking. She does.

"I thought you're moving so slowly because ye canna walk."

At her comment, the lycans hoot. Mackenzie does too.

"Well, I am sore, but that's not why I'm moving slowly." Actually, I'm not moving slowly. She's walking like she's racing a hare. Also, I dislike having this conversation out in public. The wolves have excellent hearing, and they're listening, some with their ears twitching.

"A princess walks," I say. "She doesn't run or rush."

Mackenzie blinks. "No shite?"

"A princess doesn't curse either."

"Good thing I ain't one."

"But you are."

She frowns, then widens her eyes. "Oh, I guess you're right. Never thought of meself as one." Waving her arm about her, she shouts, "Get out of the way, ye wretched peasants."

Oh no. I open my mouth to correct her, but the wolves snicker and part before us, even bowing.

Mackenzie winks, indicating a joke. "At your royal pace, Princess."

She extends her hand, indicating that I should enter the den first. It's dark beyond the group of naked males, and although these people seem playful and more relaxed than the fae, who follow protocols when entering a room where we'll dine, they are also fierce, and the fierce are also brave.

I can't show that I'm afraid of the dark.

Mackenzie's eyes soften. "It's my turn to apologize. I'm excited to finally have you around, and in all the excitement, I've made you ill at ease."

"Not at all." I square my shoulders.

She touches a finger to her nose. "We smell fear." She offers me her hand, and when I take it, she leads me into the wolves' den.

The hallway, or whatever they call this, is pitch-black, and I can't see where I'm going. I rely on Mackenzie to walk me through it. Besides the heavy breathing of the lycan males filing in behind us, it's eerily quiet. I glance behind me and startle at the sea of bright blue eyes. The males are just breathing, but because the sounds they make are almost like growling, they're scaring me.

"Princess," Mackenzie says into the silence, "you must know the males would not dare touch a strand of your hair."

"Thank you."

"My brother is an Alpha. Do you understand?"

"I think so."

"I don't think you do, or you wouldn't be so afraid."

The darkness disappears almost instantly, making me think the entrance is spelled, because we appear at the door of a large dining area. Is it a ballroom? Maybe just a dining hall or a throne room where parties are held? It is a circular room full of lycans sitting at long rectangular tables.

The entire room stills as I walk inside.

I don't know what else to do besides be the princess, even if I'm not one. I raise my hand and wave as I would greet Father's soldiers. "Good morning."

They don't respond. More than one of them turns up their noses, flares their nostrils.

They continue staring. I'm used to stares, though not as intense as the ones the lycans are throwing my way. I'm also not used to seeing this many bare-chested males wearing only sweatpants or a tied cloth covering their middle. They were all nude outside.

They're grabbing clothes from the pile on the floor next to the entrance. It appears the clothes are for everyone. Lenox must think me ridiculous for choosing mine with care.

"Let's eat." Mackenzie speeds over to a long wooden table lined with massive clay pots, out of which are sticking different utensils. At the start of the table, males are picking up ceramic plates and moving down the line, seemingly serving themselves food from the pots.

It smells delicious, and my belly growls again.

Mackenzie hands me a plate, and I follow her lead, noticing that nobody is lining up behind me and the ones in front of us are scurrying away.

"I don't bite," I whisper.

"We do, and we can't be tempted," a male says.

"Speak for yerself," another male says. "I'm not at all tempted."

Mackenzie scoops up eggs, then licks the common spoon and waves it around. "Ye all are a bunch of kittens. My brother isn't here, and none of ye even introduced yerself."

"Is that a dare?" The male we passed in the hallway walks right up to me and leans in. I lean back, but he follows, a smirk on his youthful face, a playful glint in his eye.

When I can't lean back anymore, he brushes his rough cheek against mine and sniffs. He pulls back, his eyes blazing. "It's like sniffing my Alpha's balls."

The dining hall erupts in laughter.

Embarrassed and put off, I struggle to find them amusing, turn away from the male and grab a ladle. My hand shakes.

Not only am I upset, but I've also never used a ladle before, having never served myself breakfast. I miss Marybell. I miss my court. I even miss the estate.

A hand grips mine and helps me ladle up the food.

I look up into the eyes of a very handsome male with cropped dark hair and the blazing blue eyes of his wolf.

"May I?" He offers to fill my plate, so I give it to him.

Once the plate is full, he hands it back to me and bows. I pick up on the ease with which his body folds and the grace with which he offers to escort me to an empty table.

Mackenzie follows, and with her eyes on the male, she almost trips over her feet as we sit down. Eyes narrowing, she presses her lips together.

Given how Mackenzie approached the group of males outside the dining hall and inside it, I didn't think she held back her comments. Though she does with this wolf, and there's something about him. Something very...dominant.

For some reason, it makes me feel safe.

He won't touch me or let others touch me.

Lenox wouldn't let any of them mistreat me.

And I know he wouldn't because when he steps into the dining hall, the male who helped me with the meal walks away. Every male in the room sniffing around me scatters, and silence falls as if the room is empty.

There are over three hundred males in here.

At the entrance, Lenox pauses, feet shoulder-width apart, arms flexing. He wears a sage-green kilt, no shirt, and he's barefoot, his loose hair tucked behind his ears.

I want to lick him.

"Princess," he greets me.

"Lenox," I say, breathless, as if we're the only people in the room.

"At ease, everyone," he says.

"Welcome back, Alpha!" They shout as one and stand, clapping and whistling, catcalling, throwing profanities at him. They're talking about smelling his balls on me as if it's a normal thing to say around breakfast. When Lenox shakes his head and laughs with them, I realize that perhaps I am easily offended, and instead of taking offense, I should learn about lycan customs.

Indeed, I have much to learn. Much more than I anticipated.

It's never more obvious that I haven't a clue how lycan society works than when Lenox grabs a meal and sits at a small table tucked away from everyone. A glance at Mackenzie shows me she's not finding it unusual that her brother, my mate, sits by himself.

A few moments later, I figure out why.

He's not sitting by himself.

Not at all.

19

LENOX

"Did you have a nice vacation?" the clan launa asks me as she approaches my table.

I roll my eyes. "You damn well know it wasn't a vacation."

"I don't know, Alpha." She pecks me on the cheek and lingers there, letting me sniff out her dominance. Launa is the title given to the Alpha female of my clan. Kenna and I grew up together. I gave her most of the scars on her face and body until she gave up fighting me for dominance and submitted.

Or at least I thought she submitted. She was biding her time.

Still, she's the launa of the clan, and most of the males in the clan either fear her or beg at the altar of her Alpha pussy, the only Alpha pussy within half a cycle's travel.

"Have a seat," I offer, and she nods, thanking me.

Often, I eat alone so that the clan can shoot the shite without me present, and also because I have a lot on my mind and the time I spend dining is the time I spend thinking.

Kenna gets right to it, as Alphas often do. "Did Alistair tell you I'm looking for you?"

I nod. "I figured we could eat and chat."

"We could." She shoves a piece of bread into her mouth and chews loudly.

I glance at my lass, who picks through her food and puts tiny pieces in her mouth. Different from us. Refined. Raised at the table with utensils. We eat with our teeth and claws ripping through the flesh of our fresh kill.

As if she senses me, Gloriana looks up. Smiling, I wink at her.

She sticks her tongue out at me and scoots over in front of my sister so I can't see her from my position.

What in the name of fine red behind just happened?

Turning, Mackenzie smirks like the little, evil instigator she can be. She's up to no good.

I return my attention to Kenna, who rips the meat off the chicken bone and points the bone in the direction of my mate. "I saw that. Your princess is a brat."

"I love brats." I most certainly do not.

Kenna pops the bone into her mouth and crushes it with her canines, blue-gray eyes returning to me. "A ship with a group of Kilseleians tried to leave the docks."

During the time the savage horde pillaged Kilselei and dethroned Gloriana's father, many people fled. Some of them ended up on my shores seeking shelter and a new life. Most of them are the former king's magic miners who are merely trying to survive now. Some of them are miners Gloriana will have to identify.

"And?" I ask Kenna.

"I don't care one way or the other, but the Kilseleians think we sank the ship and killed everyone who tried to leave."

Maybe we did. Those were the orders I gave, and Kenna doesn't know about them. Although the people can return to Kilselei now, most of them choose to stay on my lands. The king taxed the people heavily, and most of them who docked knew only poverty and harsh living conditions. It's different in my clan's lands, and now that their princess is mine, they will have one of their own at the top of the hierarchy. If they accept her as their ruler, I will take care of her people as I do mine. As I will take care of Kenna, even if it will break my heart to kill her.

"There have been squabbles in the bars between us and the Kilseleians," she says.

I lean back to glance at the princess, but my sister's back blocks the view. "Why did they want to leave?"

"I'm probing the males for information. Besides, you know how I feel about Kilseleians living with us and not pledging loyalty to the pack."

The Alpha female thinks the thousands of refugees we've taken in should pledge loyalty to the clan and come under my authority instead of forming their own communities. I agree. It's just that I don't want them to pledge their loyalty to me. I want them to pledge to my mate, for when I come after Kenna and those loyal to her, in case I die, I want my princess to have her people at her back.

Gloriana is here now, and one would think I would find it in me to deal with the matters of clan and docks and lands, but all I can think about is what she's hiding from me and what makes her have nightmares. I assume the worse.

I also assume responsibility for what happened to her. For what the miners did to her.

I think Kenna paid them.

I need proof.

"Alpha," Kenna bites out, using her own Alpha female

voice. I snap my attention to her and growl, disliking her tone.

She throws up her arms. "You're distracted."

"The princess is driving me crazy."

The female Alpha smirks, the scar over her eye making it close almost completely. "Finally, a female to shake you up."

"I didn't think mating would be this way."

"Which way?" She drinks her milk and wipes the mustache away with the back of her hand.

"That it would completely occupy my thoughts and time. I thought it would be...easier."

"It would be if she were a wolf."

And there it is. The problem I believe Kenna has with the princess. The princess is not a wolf. "But she's not." Kenna can't stand to have lost her position to her. My princess comes second only to me in the clan.

Leaning back, Kenna says, "I'll handle the Kilseleians as I have been doing in your absence."

This is the last time she and I will speak. Next time, we will fight. "Thank you."

She levels me with a stare. "But trouble is stirring, and sooner or later, you will have to step in."

"When it gets hot, I will. Until then, handle it."

Kenna bites her lip and averts her gaze.

"Is there anything else?" There is. I can feel it.

"You know I wouldn't say anything if I didn't think it will become an immediate problem."

"Yes?"

"Duane is training for a challenge."

I crack my neck and open my mouth to reply, just as the princess and my sister stand. She doesn't even look at me as she leaves the dining hall, and the way she carries herself with her nose slightly turned up and her feet stomping instead of stepping gracefully as I know she does tells me she's upset.

Who upset her? My sister must've stirred the pot.

They leave, and my gaze lands on Duane, whose focus lingers on the exit. He licks his lips before he stands and makes his way out. A warning growl rises from my chest, and soon, the dining hall falls silent.

Duane stops stalking my mate and turns toward me.

Standing calmly, I make my way to him, then clap him on the shoulder. He's younger than I am, and most females find him more attractive. They find me a bit too dangerous, too rough, too male, if there ever were such a thing. My sister told me that, so I believe it. She has the ears of the females in the town.

"Going somewhere?" I ask.

"I'm on the docks for the first shift."

I steer him into the tunnel before the dining hall. "I hear there's trouble at the docks," I say.

Duane nods. "You hear well, but you don't see."

I squeeze his shoulder. "What's that mean?"

"It means you haven't been around and seen what's going on for yourself."

The young wolf might be looking out for me. He might have uncovered Kenna's plot, but can't accuse her with no proof. We could be in the same boat, figuratively speaking. Or he could be challenging me.

"And what *is* going on?" I ask.

"Come to the docks with me and find out."

"Done." At the exit of the tunnel, we squint and allow our eyes to adjust to sunlight.

Pausing, I search for the princess in the meadow and monitor the males whose gazes stray toward her and her little skirt and those long legs that keep stomping. She's not moving toward the room, and I'm wondering why. Where else would she go besides our bedroom?

I'm buying her a cage.

Duane taps my hand. I realize I haven't let go of his shoulder. I've dug my claws into his flesh.

Before I rip out his arm, I step away from the wolf. Blood seeps from the holes my claws made in his shoulder, but Duane pretends as if it's a bug bite. Even though we heal faster than most creatures, the claw jabs have still got to hurt.

"I see the docks will have to wait," he says and jerks his head toward my princess.

"Duane." I move in, our chests touching. "The next time you see my mate, if your eyes are not on her fucking toes instead of her face, I will claw them out. Acknowledge."

He smirks. "Yes, Alpha."

"Good. And Duane? I'm ready whenever you are." I'm telling him I know about the challenge.

"I hope it doesn't come to that."

"But it might."

"It might." Duane nods and walks straight for the stables, in the opposite direction to where my mate is going.

"Wait for me," Alistair, one of the clan omegas shouts, and runs after my mate and my sister.

Whatever for? Where are they going? Why don't I know where my mate is going? This bothers me immensely. I should know where my mate is at all times.

As males pour out of the hall I greet them. Some pause for a chat, while I monitor the situation in the meadow like a bird of prey circling his nest.

Leading one of my favorite horses by the reins, Duane

walks out of the stable, and the moment my princess sees him, she changes direction and starts walking toward him.

WHAT IN THE ACTUAL FUCK?

I move too.

They exchange a few words, and Duane is not looking at her toes. Instead, he sees me coming and drops to one knee for the princess to step on and mount the horse.

She glances briefly toward the forest, then shouts, "Ya!"

The horse takes off as if someone smacked his behind.

The horses hate our animal form, and the moment she disappears into the trees, I have enough brain cells left to stop me from sprouting fur and teeth before I sprint after her, the laughter of my clan mates at my back.

20

GLORIANA

Where I come from, males are more discreet about their indiscretions. Even my father, the king, never shamed the presiding queen with another female. He was even discreet with his mistresses, and during formal outings, the only female by his side was either me or the queen.

Instead of dining with me, however, Lenox ate breakfast with a female who appears to be the lover he's had since forever. Mackenzie called them the Alpha pair and said her name is Kenna. They've been a pair since they were kids.

Clearly, in the clan, the wolf males do as they please, and I imagine the Alpha does whatever he wants, setting an example for all to follow, which means if I confronted him about it, in the end, my actions would only hurt me as they have since the time Father punished me for standing up for myself.

I better say nothing.

I won't say anything.

But I also won't dine with the clan anymore.

I'm unsure if I'm upset that he embarrassed me so

publicly, or if I'm hurt that I believed all the lies he told me. Either way, only a naive young idiot would believe all the mating insta-devotion the wolf claims he feels for me anyway.

I miss Marybell.

I want my life back.

I want a court where I know the rules.

I hate the wolf!

Tears fall from my eyes as I ride the white stallion through the path in the forest, letting him dictate his own way since I have no direction in mind besides getting away as quickly as possible. It seems the horse knows the path and doesn't need my guidance.

I hold on to his mane and clamp my thighs around him, securing my seat.

"Gloriana!" a male calls after me.

I click my tongue, urging the horse faster.

The stallion responds.

He's a large, strong animal.

Dense trees make me have to bend to avoid being whipped by the low-hanging branches.

As the stallion stretches out beneath me, the wind whistling in my ears, I'm starting to regret starting this horse race. White-knuckled, I clutch the mane and duck low as branches whip by overhead. The horse seems to misunderstand my body movement and accelerates.

We're on a descent, so he's even faster.

Too fast.

Maybe riding out wasn't such a great idea.

Maybe I should've saddled the horse first.

Maybe we'll never return to the den.

Fear grips me.

I'm going to die.

Oh no. Oh no. What did I do? I don't want to die.

The horse is too fast, I can barely see anything, and my arms are tiring, my fingers cramping as they twist tighter in the mane. I can't hold on much longer. I must hold on.

"Hold her down."

"Hold her down."

The fourth miner is unbuckling his belt, wrapping the metal end around his fist. He pulls back his hand and strikes!

The blur of a dark mass hits me and knocks me off the horse.

I scream at the top of my lungs as I roll down the decline, sure I'll hit my head on a rock and die.

Yet, I hit nothing, and as my momentum slows, I realize I'm wrapped within a large muscular body covered in fur. At the bottom of the decline, we stop rolling, and I gasp for breath while a loud heartbeat drums against my ear that's pressed against his chest.

I quiet down.

Calm.

And I listen to his heartbeat, which is unlike the beating of mine. It has a different rhythm, a much faster one.

I rub my cheek against his furry chest and dare to open my eyes. I inhale the scent of werewolf. Part animal, part male.

"I'm okay," I tell him. The lycan tightens his hold on me. "I am okay, right?" I ask, just to be sure this isn't heaven and I've died.

The lycan grunts.

He strokes my back, probably as a gesture of comfort, but I keep wanting to inhale his scent and bury my face in the fur on his chest. I rub my cheek on his coat again, and heat flares in both my cheeks and my insides. Somehow, I'm aroused.

Looking down at me are piercing blue eyes in a furry face. The tooth-filled muzzle shrinks as I watch. Lenox takes up his male form, hair mussed, eyes still those of a lycan.

He grinds his jaw and speaks through clenched teeth. "What the fuck was that, Princess?"

Oh, he wants to argue, does he? I push away from him, but he holds me tightly. "Let me go."

"No."

"Yes."

"No."

"Fine. You want to fight?"

He snorts. "I don't fight females."

"You fuck them."

He tilts his head in that wolfy, animalistic, adorable way. I ignore the cuteness of this confused, grown, sexy male, because I am still upset with him.

"I want to hear how you will explain your behavior"—his voice steadily rises as he continues—"and I can't let you go for fear you've lost your mind and will jump off the cliff."

I dislike upsetting him, but I'm not a pushover either. "You have some balls, wolf. To get upset with me when you took my virginity this morning, then went around with your mistress as if I didn't exist."

"Excuse me?" He rears back, wide-eyed and shocked.

"Oh, please," I say. "Quit the offended act. No reason to deny it. I'm not stupid."

He sits up, then stands, offering me a hand.

I rise on my own.

"I am offended," he says.

"Aww, I'm sorry." I wipe my hands on my torn dress. There are claw marks all over it, and my breast is exposed. "I'm really sorry—not—to have brought up your mistress, but I won't be shamed so publicly!"

"Watch your tone."

"Fuck you." I fix my dress over my breasts, but the straps are torn and the dress falls. I try again, and the front folds over my belly, leaving my nipple shrinking from the cold.

The wolf takes notice and steps toward me.

I walk backward.

"Oh, lass, I love the chase. Go on and run, see how far you get before I take you down and fuck you in the dirt."

"You wouldn't."

"I would."

My back hits something hard, and I touch it with my hands. It's a tree trunk.

The wolf pins me against it with his body.

Between his legs, he's hard. As Lenox bends his head to kiss me, I give him my cheek. "Don't."

He pecks my cheek and trails kisses down my jaw and my neck. A hand covers my breast, and I groan before I grab his wrist to still his movement.

He bites my neck, not as hard as he had when he marked me, but hard enough.

My pussy spasms at his bite, and liquid heat starts leaking out of it and down my thighs. I didn't think anyone could be this aroused.

"I never knew," he says, "that a Stenan female could respond to mating the way a wolf female might, but I'm guessing Natra made you especially for me."

"Your ego is a creature of its own. Did anyone ever tell you that?"

"No."

"It needs a name."

"Give it a name, Princess."

"Asshole."

He lifts my breast and licks my nipple, then looks up as

he puts it in his mouth and sucks. His hand sneaks behind my neck and holds me immobile while he sucks on my breast as a baby might.

It feels wrong and arousing at the same time. Lenox sure knows how to handle a female, and when he's like this, sexy and dominant and male, I stand no chance of rejecting his advances.

"I hate you," I tell him.

He unlatches from my breast and spins me around. "Hands on the trunk and spread your legs."

I don't even think about it. I do as he says, my brain catching up with my body after I'm facing the trunk. "I'm upset with you," I tell him, and start to put my hands down.

"Hands up, lass," he orders in a voice that brooks no argument. His palm lands on my belly, and he spreads his long, claw-tipped fingers.

His massive cock slides against my entrance. That's the only warning I get before he enters me from behind. He grabs my throat, a claw under my chin forcing my head to tilt back. Slowly, he moves inside me, the back of my head resting on his chest, my gaze on the evergreen tree.

"Now, lass," he says, voice deep, words deliberately drawled out to sound sexier. "Tell me what's wrong."

Nothing is wrong now. I'm full of his cock, and it feels amazing. My insides were burning, and his cock is perfectly cold and hard. It doesn't hurt as much as it did this morning. Even though I'm sore, it feels good.

"I can't remember." I can, but I like how he makes me feel. He's messing with my head.

"Good. It is not worth remembering. You and I are the only ones who matter right now. Our bond grows stronger as we spend more time together, and coupling is always the best way to build a strong mating bond."

"You have another female," I manage to say.

His fingers tighten around my throat. "I have only you. You are mine as I am yours, and no other exists for me."

"I know what I saw," I rasp. He's fucking me faster, and still, I want more of his cock. I bend forward, and when I do, Lenox grabs my hair. Yanking me back up, he pistons into me.

"Let go, Princess."

"I'm not holding on to anything," I say, breathless.

"You are," he whispers in my ear. He releases my hair, but I keep my head tilted back and rest it on his shoulder, seeking the hand on my throat without asking for it. Lenox grips my neck again, fingers splayed around it.

"How do you not trust me, but you bare your throat for me?"

"I don't know."

My locks bounce on my face, my gaze on the sun fighting through the branches of the dense forest. It smells like rain.

"Let go of the past," he says, "and welcome me as your future. I promise if you do, I will not fail you. I will honor our mating, our sacred bond. A lycan mate never cheats. It is not possible. Cheating is for men, and I am not a man. I am a wolf, the most loyal creature there ever was. To my mate, to my clan, to the land we stand on."

Lenox grabs my hips and moves me over his cock as if I weigh nothing. My hair flies around my face, my breasts bounce up and down, and my palms scrape the rough trunk.

A claw touches my clit, and I scream as the orgasm takes hold of me, makes my muscles cramp, my body freeze up while my channel undulates in ways that make me think its milking his cock for seed. And maybe it is, because Lenox comes with a shout and slaps his palms against the trunk. His claws dig into the wood and rip off the bark.

Then suddenly, he's gone, the warmth of his body at my back lost.

Leaning my forehead against the tree, I shiver.

My knees shake and fold, and so I kneel facing the tree. I look over my shoulder.

Lenox is still there, a hand on his cock, fisting the base of it and hissing as if in pain.

"You were also riding when I first saw you," he starts, black hair falling over his face when he looks up. "I was in Kilselei meeting with your merchants for a trade deal." He smiles as he tilts his head all the way back, exposing the cords of his wide neck. While Lenox takes a moment, remembering or just dealing with whatever he's dealing with now, I marvel at his physique. The defined muscles, the sheer strength of his male form makes me think Lenox is made for hunting, killing, and fucking.

The goddess has been generous with this male. And perhaps she has been generous with me too. I can't seem to see the generosity at this time, when everything I've ever known has been taken from me, and I'm doing my best to find my footing in this new life Lenox brought me into.

"After the meeting," Lenox says as he cracks his neck and shakes out his shoulders. He sits on the ground, then grabs me and pulls me into his lap.

Oh boy. When he does this, it's so comforting and nice, it makes me want to live on his lap forever.

"One of the miners offered me a secret deal and invited me to Lyan." Lenox moves my hair away from the back of my neck and kisses the place he marked.

Every time he touches the marked place, my heart skips a beat.

This wolf makes it very hard to hate him for any reason whatsoever. He can be both caring and demanding, a deadly combination for a male. One I find irresistible. I don't know what I feel for him, but hate is not it, and I'm lying to myself if I keep trying to dislike him.

I like him very much.

"I went, and there I met your late father, who signed a deal with me and invited me to hunt on Mount Havensi. He was very proud of his land and that stretch of forest."

"Kilselei is beautiful."

"Not as beautiful as Lycana."

I chuckle.

He wraps his arms around me and pulls me into his warm body.

"One morning, I hunted in the woods and slowed down as I approached what looked like someone's property at the edge of the forest. A castle, it seemed. Not large enough for a king, but just big enough for a princess."

"Blue façade with golden rooftops?" I ask.

"That's the one. Right before I was about to continue on two legs instead of four, a stableboy started shouting. You see, there was this young princess riding a stallion twice the size of what she ought to ride, racing toward the forest.

"The stableboy and other guards joined him as they ran after her. I couldn't allow her into the forest, so I stayed in wolf, knowing the horse would turn away. That's what happened, and eventually, they caught the horse.

"I thought she would be scared, but she laughed and laughed as the stableboy helped her dismount. She left for the small palace in the country, not realizing the wolf creature at the edge of the forest had just fallen in love."

21

LENOX

There. I said it. The word that makes the world spin. Love. I've never said it to anyone else, not even my sister, and definitely not to my mother or my father.

I've never loved anyone the way I love my mate. This kind of feeling cannot be replicated. It is as fierce as it is kind, a one-in-a-million chance, a divine bond many lycans will never experience.

Gloriana slowly turns and pats her messy hair, which is sticking every which way. I've never seen her quite so wild looking. She's a princess. Always perfectly groomed, perfectly charming and minding her manners, but I like seeing her with messy hair and torn dress, her breast still hanging out begging for me to suck it again.

Everything about this moment is intimate, a way for me to see her in a light others don't.

"I remember," she says.

"Huh?"

She tries fixing her clothes, but gives up with an

annoyed huff. "Castle Sentinia. Is that where you first saw me?"

I nod, stupefied. The encounter was too brief. She didn't even look at me. The horse was galloping, and she wasn't paying attention to the forest.

"I didn't know the wolf was you. Until now." She grabs my wrist and lifts it so she can measure our hands against each other. The substantial difference in the size makes her smile. "In my nightmares," she says, and I sit up, "the miners scatter when the wolf with obsidian fur barges into the room."

Mmhm. That's me. The big bad wolf. I tap my chest. "In wolf, my fur is black with silver tips."

She nods, her expression dreamy. "I painted you standing at the edge of the forest."

She painted me! I struggle to remain cool and collected when I really want to jump up and down in joy. Alpha males can't be seen hopping around like rabbits, so I say, "Really?"

Fuck, I sound like the princess.

She nods. "Really. I wish I could show you. It's a beautiful painting. Marybell hung it above my bed."

"Your bed?"

"Oh." Her eyes grow wider, and her fingers fly to her lips. "It just occurred to me it's the painting hanging on the wall of my bedroom."

"Sounds about right."

Gloriana fists her red dress. "But I'm still upset with you, lycan."

"Lenox."

"Lenox."

She says my name like she's saying something decadent and sexy. I want to fuck her again. "Are you sore down there?"

"A little. More from riding than from...you know."

"Fucking."

She nods shyly.

"Tell me why you're still upset."

"You were dining with another female."

The princess is jealous. What a fantastic span I'm having here. Rawr. I feel like biting something. "Her name is Kenna. She's an Alpha female of my clan. Often, the Alphas dine alone and apart from others so that the clan mates can have their break without feeling like we're lording over them."

"It looked like you were a couple."

"That's ridiculous."

"Not to me," she bites out.

I frown, wondering how much about wolf dynamics she's familiar with. It would not occur to a female wolf to worry about Kenna and me. "A male and female Alpha are repulsed by each other's mating scents. We would not mate." I shiver just thinking about it. "Ever."

It's Gloriana's turn to frown. "What do you mean?"

She doesn't know. Why would she know? She's a Kilseleian princess and I'm a lycan, and we have so much ground to cover. This won't be our first misunderstanding, I'm certain of it. I better learn how my princess views the world and do so quickly. I also need to educate her on our ways.

"I didn't understand what happened with you in the dining hall because the dynamics of the clan are so natural to me, and I thought you would sense it or know it. My mistake. I will ask my sister to shadow you and tell you about the inner workings of the clan. We will start with the basics."

"Which are?"

"Alpha-Alpha pairings repel. The launa's scent is dominant, and it doesn't arouse me. My scent signals to her that we should not touch."

"But you would touch other females?"

"My mate. I would touch her." I peck Gloriana's plush lips. "And luckily for me, my mate is a lass whose submissive nature suits me." I grab the back of her neck and tilt her head so I can deepen the kiss, and soon, Gloriana is under me, her ankles crossing at my back. In the back of my mind, I'm reminding myself that she's sore, and if I want to fuck her some more tonight, I can't fuck her now or after lunch or for the duration of the span until then.

I really can't.

"You're sore," I say, though it sounds suspiciously close to a whine. I do not whine. I speak. I clear my throat. I'm annoyed I can't fuck her and must restrain myself, but it's for the best, and if there's one thing an Alpha male does best, it's to take care of what's his. My mate is mine to care for. "But you could sit on my face and ride it."

Gloriana bites her lip, her blush so cute, I just want to eat her up. I push on because I like making her uncomfortable in this way. "What's a good little lass say when she wants something from the wolf?"

"Please, wolf," Gloriana whispers and averts her gaze.

I lift her chin, making her look at me. "You can beg so sweetly. Do it, lass. Beg the wolf for his fat tongue."

"Please, wolf, let me sit on your face and ride it," she says.

I flip us over and grab her bottom, lifting her. She yelps when I move her and position her pussy right over my mouth. I inhale the sexy feminine scent of my mate's pussy... and my knob end swells again, balls filling with seed. Groaning, I squeeze my sac before spreading Gloriana's arse cheeks wide and flicking her clit for a few moments, long enough for her liquid heat to drip on my chin. I swipe it with my thumb and lick. Mmhm.

Nice.

I lift her higher so I can see her pussy. It's gaping open, waiting for my fat cock and the knob end it'll get later tonight. I stick out my tongue and flick her clit again, then wait for her pussy to make me some liquid. Sure enough, her good little pussy is my soldier too. Clear liquid trails out of it, and I open my mouth to catch it right on my tongue. Mmmm.

"You're a dirty lass," I say and drop her pussy over my face, letting it gag me.

THE SUN IS OVERHEAD, just above the spot Gloriana and I occupy on the dirt. I keep her warm and draped over my body while she talks about her life in Kilselei, leaving out the parts that I'd love to know more about.

As an Alpha, I can sense when people are evading and avoiding something. I can also sense trauma, although that's not an Alpha male thing, it's a me thing. I've had experience with dealing with clan mates, including females, going through trauma.

They just want to be heard.

Acknowledged.

Have their feelings validated, especially by a figure they consider a leader of their pack.

And so I shut up and listen.

My mate talks about her father often, much less about her mother, and I get the impression we were both abandoned by our mothers. Her mother sounded too busy trying to please her father to notice Gloriana, and my mother was too busy whoring so she could buy the various herbs she used to hallucinate her way through life.

I stroke Gloriana's locks. They're pretty and soft as our baby's bottom will be.

My ears twitch at the sound of footsteps. A four-legged creature is approaching. Must be one of my patrol males.

"Keep away," I growl.

In my arms, Gloriana startles. "Is someone here?"

I keep listening for the wolf's footsteps to retreat. They don't. In fact, the wolf shifts and is now approaching on two feet.

I move Gloriana to the side and stand, cracking my neck. "This better be important."

I sniff out my sister before I see her.

"What are you doing alone in the woods?" I ask.

"I came to check on Gloriana."

"She's with me."

"I see that, genius."

"For fuck's sake, Mackenzie, why did you not explain how Alpha-Alpha relations work in a pack?"

A coy but evil smile brightens my sister's face. "I had to see what you'd do."

"That's not very nice," Gloriana says.

"I know," Mackenzie says. "I'm sorry. I was playing."

"Some of the submissive wolves are playful," I explain. "It is in their nature, though that doesn't mean I have to find it funny or appropriate. It means I have to discipline them."

"You don't discipline females." Mackenzie sticks her tongue out.

"Oh, he does," Gloriana says, then slaps a hand over her mouth.

I blink.

Mackenzie makes a face. "Gross. But you two are good now, yes?"

"Why?"

"Because there's trouble at the docks."

"Duane?"

She nods. "Come see."

Mackenzie walks toward the edge of the forest and onto the same cliff I'd feared Gloriana might topple from. We view the town set in the valley below surrounded on three sides by mountains and one side by sea, the position making it secure and nearly unreachable.

I used to come here as a boy, wondering if my mother ever looked up to try to spot me. There were times I would wave and shout at random people, and whoever raised their hand back to me, I would pretend it was her.

Then I grew up and stopped giving a shite.

She ought to have loved me. That's what mothers do.

"It's beautiful," Gloriana says.

The wind carries smoke, and I search for the source in the woods first. The trees aren't burning. Thank fuck for that. In the town, nothing seems amiss either. "Where is Duane?"

"At the docks."

"Burning ships?"

"Just one"

I curse.

"Whose ship is it?" Gloriana asks.

I won't tell her that her people are down there. I can't have my princess involved until I've secured the town.

"Mac," I say in the voice I use when giving orders.

My sister perks up instantly.

"Take Gloriana back to the den. Have her wash up and dress, then wait for my return."

"Yes, Alpha."

I address my mate. "Stay in the chambers."

She barks at me like a dog.

Shocked, I stare unblinking.

Mackenzie starts laughing so hard, she's bending over.

Damn brats. "I mean it, lass. Stay. In. The. Chambers."

22

LENOX

I've always thought there was nothing more satisfying than running through the forest on four legs. I revel in the damp ground under my paws, the sounds of small animals that scurry off to hide as I race between the trees, the smell of rain and rotting leaves in autumn, the shade the trees provide in summer, the bitter cold of forest frost in winter, and the scent of wildflowers in spring.

Sharing the forest with Gloriana is better yet, a feeling that makes me want to write songs about the wolfen goddess and praise her for giving me such a sexy mate.

When I first met my princess, during the dinner with the savages, she came across as a superficial little rich brat with not a care in the world for anyone besides herself. Granted, she *is* a rich brat, and it's unfair to find fault in her for being raised a princess. But I'm wondering if she's willing to give more of herself for her people and for us as a mated pair.

Since I'm an Alpha of my clan, she'll take on responsibilities that I presume she's unused to. I expect some of her training will kick in. After all, her father was a power-hungry male who had to have trained his daughter to ascend a throne. Not his throne, because he would never give it up willingly, but a throne, nonetheless.

Before the savages took back their rights and defeated him, and before I claimed Gloriana as mine, her father planned to marry her off to Prince El'jah. While not a king, he could have been conspiring with Gloriana's father to overthrow his brother, King Et'enne. The fae aren't exactly known for their loyalty.

Unlike the wolves.

The wolves are loyal.

And when they're not, the wound cuts deep into the clan and spreads like a disease that, if left unattended, will fester and kill us all.

When I went to retrieve my mate, I left a festering wound in my clan.

And now my clan is divided.

If Kenna were a male, I would already have dealt with the issue, but she is a female, and an Alpha female among wolves is a rarity, one I was trained and raised to shield from harm. Oftentimes, I wonder if, when the time comes, I'll be able to carry out her sentence. In the past, when she challenged me for leadership of the clan, I would subdue her and make her show me her belly if we were in wolf form, or kneel if we were fighting on two legs.

Not this time.

This time, I'll end her.

She poses a threat to my mate.

With a clear head yet a heavy heart, I arrive near the bottom of the mountain at the most western point, avoiding the path people take to the docks, then veer right and reach a spot Duane uses as an observatory. It's a small clearing under a massive novemes tree whose branches, blooming with purple succulents, drape low, reaching the top of Duane's head.

He stands at the end of the clearing under the tree and watches the seas.

Out here, there's nothing but blue sea and clear horizons.

Duane hears me coming and shoulders off his backpack, then pulls out a kilt for me. He hands me several belts.

Before turning into male, I rub against the tree trunk, lift a leg, and piss on it, marking a bit here and there so other wolves aren't confused about whose territory this is.

"Thanks," I say once I'm on two legs. "Keep the clothes. I'm not going into town."

Duane grits his teeth. Once a scrawny lad, Duane grew into a broad-shouldered Alpha male with thick black hair hanging over cunning blue eyes and a jaw you could break rocks on. He's having a hard time with my authority. It's been worse since Rohan's brother passed away. He's a young wolf with lots of energy and not enough females in the clan to fuck and sate all those hormones.

Also, there aren't enough fights now because he's too strong for most males and they're starting to avoid his Alpha scent. He's itching for something. A fight with me would do the trick. Maybe he's suicidal that way.

"The situation needs dealing with," he bites out.

"I'll deal with it."

"When?"

"When I'm good and ready. Stand down, lad." Duane meets my glare with one of his own. I step closer, growling low in my throat. "Are you challenging me or my decisions? Answer carefully. You can challenge my decisions and live. You cannot challenge me and live. Which is it?"

It would destroy something inside me if I had to kill Duane, whom I've watched grow into one of the strongest lycans I've ever known. He might even be stronger than his father.

Not stronger than me, however, and if he challenges me, I'll kill him.

Besides, I need him alive to protect Gloriana and my sister in case something happens to me.

Duane averts his gaze and steps back. He rolls his shoulders, scrubs his face, and walks it off.

Giving him a few moments, I watch the boat sink.

Duane comes back to stand with me. I throw an arm around his shoulders and squeeze. "Thank you for looking out for me."

"I don't know what I'm looking out for. Before you went on your mate hunt, you asked me to watch the docks and make sure the Kilseleians were welcomed and stayed put. 'No boats with Kilseleians leave the docks' were your orders. And I've carried out those orders, multiple times."

"And?"

"I'm wondering why you asked me to police the Kilseleians when Kenna is dealing with them. She punished me for going against her orders. Several times." He pulls back his kilt and shows me an iron burn marking inside his thigh. That must've hurt.

"Did you tell her it was on my orders?"

"Hell no. I smell something rotting in the ranks."

An Alpha male would.

"Look." He lifts left foot, then his right one. "Burned my feet. I ran on burned feet for a cycle, so the least I deserve is an explanation. I won't follow you blindly anymore, Lenox. Throw a wolf a bone."

"I can't trust Kenna."

"What?" Duane whips his head toward me. "What? What do you mean?"

I chuckle. "I mean what I said. I can't trust Kenna."

Duane blinks. "She's your second."

"I have no proof, but I think Kenna paid miners to kill my mate. I think they thought my mate was dead, and now she is not. When I returned with her, I presume they sent out a boat to test the waters, trying to leave before I avenged the princess."

Duane nods. "It seemed like a merchant boat with supplies."

"The boat is irrelevant now. What is important is that the princess is here and able to identify the miners who hurt her."

"Hurt her how?"

"She won't say." I have my own demons I don't speak of, so I won't pry. They hurt her, and for that, they'll pay with their lives.

"How do you know they're here?" he asks.

"Asset retention."

"A what?"

"Assets. Kenna's assets, to be precise. She gave them safe haven, and they will help her take over the clan and live under her rule."

"This is why she's pushing for you to force them to pledge their loyalty to the clan."

"The clan Alpha," I correct, and that's where lycan laws get tricky. "When the foreign entity is pledging loyalty, the wording is specific to a single Alpha, not the clan."

"That's fucked up."

"Not entirely. The pledge was written to ensure alliances can be broken. Not all Alphas are made the same, and frankly, some bonds shouldn't last for centuries, only long enough for each party to get whatever they came for within a finite time." I pledged my loyalty to the Kilseleian king. When he died, I had no obligation to his country.

Duane sits on the ground. "I don't know what to do with this information. Will we go to war with each other?"

Traitors are rare in a clan. My father was one, and I have no tolerance for them. If only Kenna weren't a launa of the clan and a friend who used to roll in the dirt with me. We would talk about our future mates, our parents, our wounds, our future. The betrayal makes me want to tear her heart out and eat it.

Duane nudges me, and I realize I'm growling.

"It's time," I say.

"For?"

"For the clan to take sides."

"Fuck."

"Gather those loyal to me and lie in wait. When I take the princess into town to identify the miners, Kenna's wolves will be waiting. They will strike at us, the mated pair."

"Double fuck."

"Exactly. Once everyone is in town, you will close in for the kill."

Duane's magic flares, making his eyes almost white, a restless young lycan bloodthirsty for the thrill of combat. "We're trapping them."

"That's right. I just need their location."

"The tavern."

My turn to whip my head around in shock. "What?"

"Yeah, Kenna shags a pack of Kilseleians who work at the new tavern. I'd start there."

"Kilseleians don't come in packs."

"She groups them."

"Huh."

Duane shrugs. "Must be an Alpha female thing."

"Must be."

We're quiet before he asks, "How was the fae court?"

"Silly."

"I hear they have orgies all the time."

"Not all the time."

"Sometimes?"

I nod.

Duane seems introspective. "Hey, Alpha?"

"Aye?" Perhaps he will ask about his father.

"You ever do a group of females at once?"

Should've known better. "Duane, I'm a mated male."

"Sucks to be you, I guess."

"Lad, muzzle it."

He laughs, a playful twinkle in his eye. "It's good to have you back."

23

GLORIANA

M*eanwhile in the den...*

"We're not staying in your chambers," Mackenzie announces the moment we walk inside said chambers. For a while, I stare at her, stuck on the *your* part of her words. The chambers are mine. Accurate.

"I wasn't intending to stay here." I'm not a pet.

"Sadly, we are staying in the den."

"The town looked lovely."

Mackenzie shakes her head. "We'll go on lockdown soon, so you and I have to stay put. The males would go nuts if they discovered any females were out during these times."

"What times?"

Mackenzie bites her bottom lip. "I can't say."

"You can, but you don't want to."

"If Lenox hasn't said anything, I can't either."

I can feel her discomfort and the tension in the room.

She seems like a nice female, if a bit on the wild side. But I like the wild side. I've never explored mine. "It's okay." I pat her on the shoulder. "I understand what lockdown means." All too well. "One time, Father found out I snuck out of the house and had me lashed and locked inside my rooms with no baths for seventeen spans."

"Oh no. I'd go nuts." She tilts her head, reminding me of a curious wolf who comes upon something strange in the forest. "Why seventeen spans?"

"I was seventeen."

Mackenzie's eyes twinkle. "What did you do?"

"I followed the mysterious Summer Court's commander to a hotel."

Mackenzie's eyes go as wide as plates. "Commander sounds hot. What's he like?"

"Well, he's a fae male, but kind of built larger and...more rugged."

Mackenzie nods. "Like my brother. A lycan kind of hot." She makes a face. "Not that I think Lenox is hot. Gross."

"Duane?" I prompt.

"Again, gross. Duane is my cousin."

Oh. The way she looked at him earlier gave me the wrong impression.

"Go on now, don't keep me in suspense."

I nod. "What I thought was a hotel was actually a brothel."

"Juuuuuicy. Then what happened?"

"Well, the commander knew I was following him and trapped me inside one of the rooms. Alone." Shivering, I remember how he scared me. "He stood there by the window with his hair rising as if on a wind, but there was no wind. Then," I whisper, "the sheets started moving, the bed scraped the wooden floors, and the door rattled."

Mackenzie whispers, "What kind of magic is that?"

"No idea, but it scared the blood out of me."

"Then what happened?"

"He called the guards and had me escorted back to my father."

"He should've walked you home himself."

I shake my head. "That fae is a stickler for rules."

Mackenzie snorts. "Sounds like a male who needs to shag more often."

"Hence the brothel."

We laugh.

Moments later, I turn about the room, checking the walls for secret passages. Unable to find any, I ask Mackenzie. "The bathroom?"

"Outside."

"Nooooo."

"Mmmhm."

"I can't bathe outside. It's too cold. Have the staff bring us two baths, oils too."

Mackenzie laughs. "We don't keep staff, and we have underground springs."

"Perhaps we can bathe there?"

"Hmm." Mackenzie purses her lips, then smiles slyly. "Technically, those are part of the den."

The journey to the baths is as dark and as scary as the tunnel we passed on the way to the dining hall. Since Mackenzie sees in the dark and I don't, we hold hands. I hear something scraping and whining in front of me. I halt, jerking her back.

"Don't worry," she says, "it's only a really heavy door."

Dim light breaches the tunnel as the door slowly opens and we walk in, closing the door behind us. Allowing my eyes to adjust to the low light, I curl my toes. Warm water coats the gravel, and my feet sink a bit into it. I groan and shimmy out of my torn clothes. And only then do I look up and count seven interconnected bodies of water under an uneven granite ceiling lit by both wax candles and light bugs.

The baths are full of nude males. Everywhere my eyes can see are long, large penises. So many penises.

Only a few spans ago, I was a virgin who'd never seen a single male organ.

Now, not only have I seen a dick, I see dozens of them hanging between the long, hairy, muscular legs of males who seem as frozen as I am.

They're staring, and I'm staring, heat burning my cheeks.

"Never seen a pair of tits before, have ye?" Mackenzie shouts.

Seemingly waking from a stupor, the males blink and return to going about their business, every once in a while throwing glances our way.

Mackenzie pulls me with her, and we take the narrow passages between the baths to get all the way in the back.

"Couldn't we have washed up with a cloth?" I whisper hiss at her.

Gracefully, she dives into the baths while I sit on the edge and slowly immerse my body into the water. With the temperature colder than I expected, I shiver, but compared to outside, it's warm in here. Mackenzie leaves for a stack of small barrels. She reaches inside and grabs soap, then returns, handing me a bar.

I sniff. Scentless. "Do you have something with a perfume?"

"That is perfumed."

"I can't smell anything." As soon as the words leave my

month, I know why. "Because your senses are more acute than mine. What is it?"

"Evergreen magnolias."

"Never heard of the flower."

"It's a Lycana native. Grows in the forest and on the trees. Purple. Yellow. Red. This is the red one."

I imagine a tree with flowers in those colors. "That must look pretty."

"I will take you to a place sometime."

The males are drifting toward us. Slowly, they're treading the water, their blue lycan eyes like beacons of light above clear blue waters.

I dunk under water to wet my hair and lather it. I keep expecting a strong scent to hit my nose, but nothing comes. "Is there a shop in town where they make soaps for tourists?"

"There is one, but we use faint scents because stronger ones bother our noses."

"Your brother used oils on his body when we were in the Summer Court. It smelled wonderful and strong, and he didn't seem bothered."

The entire place grows silent, and I have a feeling I said something I shouldn't have. "What?" I whisper, looking around the now much quieter space.

Mackenzie draws closer. "My brother used oils on his body?"

I nod.

"While he was in the fairy court for their mating season?"

A few males start forming groups inside the baths we are occupying.

I don't answer.

"Where did you two go?" Mackenzie asks.

"Out."

"On a courting date?"

I nod.

The males snort, and it sounds suspiciously like laughter.

"What is it, Mackenzie? I feel like I'm oversharing."

"A lycan uses oils on his body when he wants to drown out his mating scent. I bet he was fending off the faries."

"My mating scent is for my mate," a voice booms in the room.

Water splashes all around us.

There are sounds of running feet shuffling over the gravel.

In an instant, the baths are empty, not a single lycan male in the space, and even Mackenzie starts moving toward the edge as if escaping.

"Mac," Lenox snaps in a voice that makes me want to click my heels together and report for duty. Damn, he's good at this Alpha thing. "You're grounded for the rest of the cycle."

"Oh, come on, brother. It was a joke."

Lenox narrows his eyes. "A joke is funny. I'm not laughing. Bringing my mate into the public baths is not acceptable. You're lucky you're female, or I would have you whipped."

Mackenzie's eyes fill with tears. "I'm sorry, Lenox. I didn't mean to disappoint you." She climbs out of the baths and grabs a towel from a nearby bench before leaving.

Lenox lands those ice-blue eyes on me. "Get out of the baths and dress." He turns and walks away, then pauses at the door, giving me his profile. His ears twitch, and then he turns his head. "Did you not hear me?"

"I heard you."

He turns slowly, his eyes ablaze. "Are yer legs injured?"

Oh boy, this is his extreme-asshole mode. "My legs are fine." I lather my hair with soap and dunk to rinse. I do this twice, leaving him practically fuming from his ears. I would never dare defy a male in power before, but Lenox won't hurt me. I know this the same way I know how to ride a horse. And while Lenox is strong and powerful, I dislike being ordered about as if I'm one of his wolves.

I also dislike confrontations and especially ones I will surely lose.

So I do what comes naturally. Seduce him. "I am dirty. Very dirty. Do you think you could help me wash?" Facing him, I hop out and sit on the gravel. Leaning back, I prop myself on my elbows and place my heels on the edge of the bath. Then I spread my legs, inviting him.

Lenox stalks over to me, ripping off his kilt as he approaches.

He's angry his males and I bathed in the same space, and his jealousy turns me on. He cares about me. He's not a suitor my father picked. Not a male who would have me for my crown or gold or status.

This lycan is with me for me, and while he might be older and more experienced, that just makes him more attractive to me. I also like that I can defy him without being punished. I know this like I know he'll execute a graceful dive, powerful body making barely a splash in the baths, swimming under the water, then coming up on my end and sticking out his big fat tongue to lick from my pucker hole all the way to my clit.

Lenox tries flipping me onto my belly, but I catch his face and kiss him, telling him in not so many words I want to look at him while he fucks me. If only this one time. I can already tell he prefers the position that allows him most control over my body. When I'm lying with my back to him.

Not this time, though.

I want to see my wolf.

He appears to be in his thirties, but he's much older. The jet-black hair that falls over his blue eyes makes me want to fix it.

And so when he pins me against the gravel, I tuck his hair behind the ear.

"You are sore," he says, and refuses to enter me.

I claw his back. "Fuck me."

He kisses my forehead. "I cannot keep my hands from you," he admits. "But I will fuck you when you are good and ready."

"I am ready." I lift my hips.

"Gloriana," he growls, although it's a bit more like a whine. "If we shag now, I will blow the knob end, and you won't be walking for spans."

"Good. Since you seem to want me sequestered in the rooms, I have no need for walking."

"It so happens I need yer help in town."

"My help?" What could he need from me?

"I need you to identify the miners that hurt you."

I gasp, cold sweat immediately washing my body. "I can't."

"You have to."

"Why?"

"Because if you don't," he whispers, "I'll kill them all."

24

GLORIANA

Back in our chambers, I'm bundled in a blanket and sitting on Lenox's lap while a male is fixing the fireplace. He's dressed in sweatpants and no shirt. "Is he not a member of household staff?" I ask, trying to understand how anything gets done around the den.

"Corey is a runt earning his rank."

By way of greeting, the male lifts a hand, but doesn't turn around.

"An orphan wolf," Lenox continues.

"That's right," Corey says. "Better here than with those two Kilseleians. No offense, Princess."

I frown.

Lenox explains. "Found him hidden in the barrels in the ship as I made my way out of Kilselei. A wealthy couple bought him when he was three years old, and he served them until the savages sacked yer capital and the house of his owners. He heard that lycans had docked at yer shores, and here he is."

"In the best lycan clan on Lycana." The male howls.

Lenox returns the call, and the male leaves, fire

burning nicely in the hearth. Moments pass, and Lenox and I share the silence. Sitting alone with him comforts me, and I feel a level of contentment that makes me think I've known this male for decades. It must be the mating bond. Near him, right now, the marking pulses on the back of my neck.

He rubs the spot as if he knows it's pulsing. "We must leave."

"At the baths, I probably heard you wrong."

"I doubt it, Princess. I speak my needs clearly."

"You said you needed my help."

"That's what I said."

Nobody has ever needed my help. Well, maybe Marybell that one time when the miner wanted her and she refused him and hid in my bedroom so he wouldn't bother her anymore, or worse, force himself on her. I had him shipped off in a few turns, and we never saw him again.

"I have a bad feeling about this," I say.

"It's because you will not like what I've done." His thumb swipes across the marking. Back and forth. Back and forth.

"What did you do?"

Lenox kisses my shoulder. "You are kindhearted, and you will forgive me." He looks up and says, "I need yer help with the Kilseleian settlers."

My heart starts pounding loudly in my ears. "I didn't realize there are settlers here."

"Some of yer people left when they couldn't pay taxes. Others left when the hordes started raiding."

I make an O with my mouth. "I had no idea Kilseleians couldn't pay taxes."

"Yer father taxed heavily. His people were poor, and after the savages conquered yer land, the boats from the Kilseleian ports were wandering over the seas. No other ruler would take that many foreigners, and after I realized you had fled my claim, I took them."

"The Stenans would take us."

Lenox snorts. "One would think, since that's where the original settlers moved from, but no. Some boats were accepted, but most were turned away. And so, I let them dock on my shores."

"That's...that is charitable. They had nowhere to go, and you took them."

Lenox sighs. "I secured yer people and brought them to my shores so that if you refused the mating, I would have a bargaining chip."

What is he saying? It takes me a moment to process what the lycan is telling me. I gasp. "You took hostages."

"That's right."

I move to leave his lap, but he holds me prisoner. "Hear me out."

"I have heard enough."

"You will listen more."

"Let me go!" I struggle on his lap, but he tightens his hold.

"When yer father called with the news that the savages had seized his city for over a cycle, I raced my boats to yer shores. My males were ready to die for you, and believe me, savages are not easy to kill. I was prepared to lose most of my clan mates so I could claim you. And then you left. You fucking left with the fairy king."

"I did not leave with the fairy king."

"Oh no?"

"No. I... I didn't know you, and I didn't know the savages. I was alone and scared."

"The new queen and the savage king would have protected you. They told me so."

"I thought I was marrying the Summer prince, and so I went to the Summer Court where I knew I'd be kept safe."

"Which is why I came, Gloriana. I would have protected you. You were not alone."

"I didn't know that."

"You didn't give me a chance. You were never a stranger to me, so when you treated me like one, I secured thousands of yer people."

I gasp again. "Thousands?" How dare he! "Let them go," I order in a voice I thought lost to me.

"Some of them touched you in ways you don't like. What ways, Princess? You can tell me."

I shake my head. "I can't."

"But you can identify them."

"I'd rather not."

"I know." He tightens his arms around me. "But if you point them out to me, I promise they will never bother you again."

He's offering a safe haven. A refuge from the nightmares. He's offering revenge.

I can't continue living my life imprisoned on the estate or even in the den. I love meeting people, and I'm unsafe if I do so when enemies are watching me, biding their time, seeking revenge against my father. Lenox kept my enemies close so he can deal with the threat in his own way on his land.

"There were four," I tell him. "They wrapped leathers around their fists and... Well, they would've pounded me into a pulp if the blond savage hadn't shown up. He killed one, but three are still at large. The healers fixed me before you came."

Lenox's body is as stiff as a frozen branch on a tree. Unmoving. I don't think he's breathing. I sit up and meet icy blue eyes. His upper lip twitches before he bares his teeth and allows me to see his growing canines and the jaw that's jutting out and becoming larger to accommodate the werewolf teeth.

He is angry for me, not at me, and I'm not scared of him anymore. I stroke his jaw. "They say a lycan bite can snap the thigh bone of an orc in half."

"Depends on the lycan."

"If I identify the miners, will you let the rest of my people leave?"

"They'll stay of their own free will."

"You don't know that."

"I do."

I frown. "How can you be sure?"

"Their princess is my mate."

"And?"

"And when they pledge to her, they will have a voice in the clan."

A voice in the clan. "I would like that for them." And for me. It sounds like a calling. A purpose. Something bigger than me, and I want the responsibility. "I'll do it, wolf."

25

GLORIANA

Lenox paces the chamber. I stare at the wardrobe's limited contents, realizing nothing is appropriate for my appearing before my people.

"I have nothing to wear." When Lenox doesn't respond, I turn and catch his gaze as he walks by me.

"Is it over yet?"

"Is what over yet?"

"Are you done deciding what to wear?"

"No," I scoff.

"How much longer?" he asks through gritted teeth.

"The clothes are unsuitable, so a long while."

He sighs and hugs me from behind, resting his jaw on top of my head. I'm nude, and he's dressed, and the coolness of his black leather kilt against the hot backs of my thighs makes me horny.

"I need gowns."

"They're on their way."

"And Marybell."

"Also on her way. In the meantime—"

"I know, I know," I interrupt. "You think I'm silly when I

fret over clothes." I pick out a dark gray dress, and after I slip it on, I notice a pair of black slippers on the floor. They're new. "Those weren't here before."

"I remembered a shipment that came in once many turns ago that had sandals. I grabbed them on the way up to the chambers. Before I found you at the baths."

I put on the slippers, a size too small for my rather big feet, and pin my hair into a tight bun, but then make it messy because it just feels right. Lenox and I exit. A male with dirt smeared on his face waits for us outside. He leads a horse, the same horse I rode already.

I fold my hands in front of me and step aside so Lenox can mount the animal as I wait for the carriage that'll take me to town, but Lenox grabs my hips and lifts me onto the animal's back. I yelp as he mounts the horse right behind me.

No carriage.

Only one horse.

Okay.

The ride to town takes longer than expected, and by the time we arrive, it's well past lunch and my stomach is growling something fierce.

Behind me, Lenox taps my belly. "We'll eat later."

"Okay." Apparently, that's the only word in my vocabulary. Although my belly growls, I can't eat. All I can think about is those miners, whose faces are becoming clearer and clearer in my mind as we approach the town.

I've never been in a town in front of people on horseback, with or without guards, and while I'm used to people stopping to stare, I've rarely been this exposed to the public. I feel underdressed and unprepared for the outing. My gowns and my tiara, I realize now, were my armor.

"Let's head back," I blurt.

"You have nothing to fear."

"They will spit on me, throw rotten fruit at me. They'll hate me like they hate my father."

"Nobody will throw anything at us, I promise you that."

On the busy streets, people going about their business part to make a path for the horse. There are no carriages or other horses, and as we descend the narrow street toward the water, my people, along with several lycans, glance our way, than do a double take, their gazes fixed on me.

Males carry swords. I wear my tiara. Without it, I am bare, scared, and vulnerable.

"Steady now," Lenox says, his voice reassuring. "These people need a princess."

"I'm not really a princess."

"You are. To me you are, and in yer heart, you are, and to yer people, you are."

"What if they reject me?" I swallow as people form lines for the horse to pass.

"They will not."

"How can you know?"

"Because those who do will be escorted off my lands."

"Seems harsh."

"Our world is harsh. Harsh is what yer father did. He mined others for magic."

I turn in the saddle and look at the wolf, who stares down his nose at me.

"You hold a grudge against my father."

"Damn right I do. Hearing that his magic came from draining creatures with both animal and male form doesn't sit well with me. Frankly, I never liked the man."

Men who don't like him want to hurt me. My heart's starting to beat too fast. I might be having a panic attack.

The lycan wraps his arms around me. "Easy now, Princess. I would never let anything happen to you."

"My father wasn't popular."

"No, he wasn't."

"Can you not understand, then, why I hid in the Summer Court?" The news of our arrival is spreading, and more people are starting to gather.

"I can, but you can't spend the rest of yer life in hiding."

"Is that what I'm doing?"

"Yes."

As we round the corner and the crowds around us grow, people start pointing fingers and whispering about the lycan Alpha and the poor young princess he forced into mating. We pass a group of Kilseleian ladies (judging by their gowns), and I overhear, *"Look at her plain dress. Poor thing."*

"They're talking about yer dress," Lenox says, seemingly shocked.

"Told you so."

The smell of fish and vomit precedes the docks, and as we round the corner, we arrive on a wide street in a busy marina where lycan males and a few Kilseleians are pushing trade carts and yelling about the various produce they're selling.

Amid the commotion, the horse slows and shakes his head, clearly as uncomfortable as I am. The exposure to the public feels brutal to me. Fear grips me, and I freeze on the animal just as Lenox dismounts. He stretches out his arms. "Come here."

I'm paralyzed. There're hundreds of strangers, mostly males, on the streets, working on the docks and boats. Without carriage and guards… "I can't."

"You can, Gloriana. Come here." Lenox gently touches

my wrist and tugs. He could pull me down, but he doesn't, giving me time to adjust.

"I didn't anticipate this many people."

"This many *men*. You didn't have a problem with the fae or the lycan males."

"That's right."

"Come here."

Reluctantly, like a child, I lower myself into his warm embrace, where I stay as he hugs me. Lenox seems to be hugging me all the time. What they say about wolves being attentive is true, but they say that about wolves who are just lovers. They don't yet know about wolves who are mates. If they're anything like mine, females around the world should be riding into Lycana wishing for a lycan mate.

Or maybe it's not all the wolves who are generous with attention. Maybe it's just mine.

He is mine.

I rear back and lock eyes with his blue ones and tell him what I'm thinking. "If the rest of the females knew how generous you are with your affection, they would try to take you from me."

"Good thing they don't know, then."

I shake my head. "You're supposed to say something along the lines of 'they cannot take you from me because I'm loyal and mated.'"

He winks. "I'm playing hard to get."

I laugh and, just like that, forget my fears.

For now.

Lenox threads his fingers with mine, and we walk the streets. Or rather, he marches while I'm trying not to step on noodles and dip my toe in a rotten tomato. Vomit, old soup, and even a waste chamber pot or two are all emptied on the streets.

We're passing the blacksmith, and the noise of several powerful shirtless lycans hammering the metal makes me cringe. Lenox waves and one of the males facing us lifts his head. He wipes his face and eyes and smiles, one eye closing shut completely.

I make a noise in the back of my throat and almost trip, but Lenox squeezes my hand tighter, and we keep walking as if nothing happened. The male sparked a memory. I don't know what. What is it? I'm trying to remember why his eye closing shut when he smiles is familiar, and when I do, I stop.

Lenox won't let me stop, though.

"Keep walking," he hisses.

"Oh, my Ensna," I whisper.

"Keep walking, Princess."

"That male..."

"I know."

"You know?" I hiss back.

Lenox takes a sharp left into a tavern, and I stop dead in my tracks. It's full of my people and not the lycan's. Most are men but there're women too, women I recognize from the Kilseleian court.

Silence falls.

They stare.

The women give me a once-over, taking in my appearance. A miner I recognize as one of the three men who... who hurt me slowly stands and starts making his way out the back door at the same time as all the men gather and form a line as if they're anticipating a fight.

"Stay," Lenox barks, but seemingly in fear of their lives, more men sneak out the back door.

Clearly, they're here and with families, because I find the other two miners sitting with younger women who could be their daughters. They're about my age, and I remember them from court.

"Margaret." I greet the woman I used to embroider with.

The pretty brunette stands and slips away from her father's grip to approach me. She curtseys. "My princess," she says. Something inside my chest blossoms again.

"You are looking well," she says. "What news of the Kilseleian court?"

"The savages have the court."

"That's too bad," she says, then glances at Lenox. The blush that spreads across her face makes it obvious she finds him attractive.

"Ladies," Lenox says, "wait outside for the princess."

The women start filing out, and a short, red-haired women says, "It's so good to know you're alive, Princess." Is it Isabel?

"Thank you. You too." She's not Isabel. I don't know her, but I would like to get to know her. In fact, I want to get to know them all. Where are these women sleeping? How did they get here? I have so many questions.

But first, my wolf has a score to settle.

The miners stay, as do most of the Kilseleian men.

Lenox leads me to the bar directly across from the door and lifts me to sit on it.

"Would you like something to drink?" he asks.

Doors slam as the miners use the opportunity to escape out the front and back.

I open my mouth to alert Lenox of their attempt, but clamp it shut when his eyes blaze so blue, they're almost white. Moments later, the miners who escaped return, looking more frightened than they were inside the tavern.

Outside, the lycans howl.

Lenox smiles, his teeth growing, his jaw unlocking and popping to make room for larger canines.

"Come at me, all ye cowards who attacked my female." Lenox starts growling, the tone of it one I'd hoped not to hear again, a low gurgling sound as if it's made by an entire pack of wolves warding off a threat that's entered their dark den. It's so frightening, even I'm getting scared.

Lenox continues, "These men bragged about attacking you, but I don't know which of them did it, because they all bragged."

I am so ashamed.

I want to hide.

"I will make them pay." Magic explodes, and a massive black-and-silver long-haired wolf animal as tall as I stands in the tavern. Tail tucked neatly between his legs, his head dips low as he peels back his upper lip to show red gums with canines the size of my forefinger.

The three miners who attacked me stand opposite the wolf, the flowing red glow of their blood magic caressing their hands.

"We had fun with the little princess," one of them says.

The wolf leaps.

The miners join hands and erect a blood shield.

"Noooo," I scream.

Too late.

The wolf's paws pierce the shield, and he howls in agony, the strong momentum of his movement pushing him forward, searing his paws, face, and body.

The shield collapses when Lenox lands on one of the miners and tears into the man's face, ripping out his cheek.

Looking away, I move to stand behind the bar. I will have that drink now. My hands shake when I grab the first bottle of something milky, and I break several glasses before I grip one firmly.

And yet, the slippery thing falls though my shaking hands.

I grab another glass, this one smaller and shorter, manageable, but it too slips though my fingers. *Fuck it,* as Marybell would say. I tilt the heavy, full bottle and chug, keeping my eyes on the ceiling. Something wet hits my face, and I wince, but keep drinking. It's a sweet alcoholic drink and goes down my throat like water.

Tables and chairs break, miners scream, Lenox is snarling and gnawing on their flesh. I put the drink down, my back facing the carnage the lycan Alpha is wreaking in the tavern.

It feels like an entire turn has passed since he attacked, but I'm certain it's only been a few moments.

When the silence falls, I realize I'm humming and rocking on the balls of my feet.

Heavy animal breathing sounds approach from behind me. I'm too scared to turn, and yet I must turn, because the lycan did this for me. He did it so I could sleep at night.

He did it because he loves me.

He ate away all my fears, and so I turn.

Before me stands Lenox in his werewolf warrior form. Half man, half wolf, with skin completely flayed off his face, arms, and belly. He is a mountain of raw exposed cords of muscle and blue eyes. Blood drips from the tips of his claws onto ripped-out chunks of scalp and dark hair spattered across the floor.

His breathing is interrupted by a gurgling sound.

He is hurt. He is badly hurt.

And yet his gaze drops to my feet and he says, "You cut yer toe."

Most people aren't lucky enough to note this moment. The moment when they fall in love with that special someone, someone they can trust with their heart, body, and soul. Lenox is that someone for me.

I look down to see that my toe is bleeding from the glass that broke when I dropped it. Lenox lifts me into his arms so I don't step on glass, or any of the body parts he left in the tavern, on our way out.

Outside, the sun shines brightly past the noon mark, and I shield my eyes. Massive lycan wolves roam the streets, not even one on two feet to be found among them. The Kilseleians seem to have vanished, likely hiding.

When Lenox emerges from the tavern, he doesn't linger, but walks back to the den, his clan of wolves following behind him.

26

LENOX

The only reason I'm not screaming my lungs out and whining like a calf left behind in the meadow is because my mate is lying next to me, and I can't have her feel sorrier for me than she already does.

Gloriana's pity is difficult to swallow, even if warranted.

I almost burned to death.

My damaged upper body feels like it's still on fire.

When I pushed my way into an active blood shield, I didn't know it could melt skin and damage muscle all the way to the bone. I'll recover only because I'm the clan Alpha who can survive and heal from injuries most lycans cannot. The magic brewing inside me is healing my body as I lie in my bed, hoping the time it takes will be quick.

Duane knows about Kenna's treason.

Froyd, the lycan Gloriana recognized on our way to the tavern, attacked Duane and as they fought, Froyd spilled about Kenna. He told Duane that Kenna is calling up her followers, and the time for an Alpha challenge has come. There're no laws saying she can't issue a challenge if I'm hurt and incapable of defending myself.

And when I'm hurt and unable to defend myself I also cannot defend my princess, and I fear Kenna will hurt her.

So it's a good thing the princess won't leave my side.

Swallowing, I open my mouth to speak, but my throat is parched and all that comes out is a wheeze.

Gloriana sits up and keeps her gaze slightly above my head, avoiding looking at me directly. I must look like I burned in the pits of seventh hell and the monster lording over it decided he'd send me back just to scare people.

"Oh, my poor wolf," she says and rubs my thigh, the part of my body where I'm still whole. From the waist down, I'm fine. It's the waist up where my own mate can't even look at me.

"I remember reading lycans heal quickly," she says, "and on their own, and since your clan brought you here and left you on your own, I think you will recover. Also, they said to lock the door and let in only the other Alpha while you're down. I don't like it, but I'm a big girl and can handle another big girl having access to my male."

Her possessive tendencies are cute.

Mine are murderous.

Kenna cannot come in here.

I try speaking again and choke on my own spit. My lungs seize, and I gasp as I attempt to expel the spit that entered a pipe it shouldn't have. Since I'm on my back, coughing proves challenging, and I'm gasping for air like a fish out of water while Gloriana leaps off the bed, a look of terror on her face.

Soon, she'll start freaking out.

She'll unlock the door and shout for help.

"Oh no, oh no, what do I do, what do I do?"

She approaches the bed, hands stretched out to help me,

but I'm fried raw and bleeding and she doesn't know where to touch me.

"Help!" she shouts.

I'm going to die choking on my own spit. What kind of miserable motherfucking lycan Alpha dies choking on his spit?

Fuck, fuck.

Gloriana disappears from view, and I hear the door open, footsteps, and Kenna comes into view.

Good. Kill me now before I die choking on my spit.

No, don't kill me, because my mate might be next.

I've lost control of the situation, and I cannot stand it. Lying here unmoving is shite.

Kenna grabs my shoulder and digs her claws into it before rolling me to my side and slamming a fist into my back. This compels my lungs to start working again, and I suck in a breath as if it's the last one I'm ever gonna take.

And maybe it is, because Kenna says, "Leave us."

I don't think Gloriana will leave.

"Did you not hear me?" Kenna asks.

Do I sound like her?

"I heard you," my mate answers, "and I'm choosing to stay."

My back is turned away from Kenna, which is the worst possible position in this case. Not only because my mate is in the same room as my enemy and I can't defend her, but because I'm not even facing my enemy.

I have never felt more helpless. Not even when my uncle took turns toughening up me and Kenna, and that was the most traumatic turn of my life. As he was beating me, I knew I would, at some point, grow into my strength and take revenge.

And so I have.

With Kenna, right now, I can't say I'll take revenge, because if she strikes, I won't have an opportunity. It's not her style to kick the already wounded, but she must be desperate by now. She knows that I know she betrayed me.

A faint noise at the door makes me want to frown. I can't frown because I can't move my raw face.

It sounds like someone is picking the lock.

Someone outside chuckles evilly, and the door opens.

"Top of the evening to you all." Rohan's voice booms in my chamber.

There's a moment of silence before Kenna responds. "Rohan?" she says, sounding as surprised as I am. He's the last lycan I expected to hear. Where is Duane?

Oh no.

Did Kenna get rid of Duane? Besides me, he's the only other member of the clan who knows about her betrayal.

I regret not telling my mate about Kenna. Gloriana would now not let her in if I had told her. Or would know to secure her life while I'm down. She would return to the Summer Court.

I never thought I'd think this, but the Summer Court sounds like the safest place for my princess right about now.

"Ladies." Rohan greets them in a flirtatious, light tone. He rounds the bed and crouches beside me so we're at eye level.

With his groomed beard and dark hair pulled back tightly at the nape, Rohan looks less like a pirate and more like the male I remember from before he left for the seas.

He gives me a once-over. "You're looking like a hairless fried single ball sac."

Thank you, arsehole.

He looks up at Kenna, then at me and winks before

standing and walking over to...to Gloriana. I hear a kissing noise.

I think he kissed my mate.

My breathing starts picking up. I'm gonna die trying to kill him.

He chuckles.

Oh, that fucker.

Fucker is fucking with me while I'm down.

Moments pass, and he's out of my view.

Oh wait, here he comes. I strain to move my eyes so I can see from the corner of them and glimpse Rohan guiding my mate to my side of the bed. By her hand. My gaze lands on their joined hands. He knows it too, because he brings them to his lips and kisses her skin, his nostrils flaring.

"Your princess smells good."

And finally, I whine.

I whine like that calf left behind in the meadow because my mind is racing, but my body can't move.

"Kenna," Rohan says, "ye have until nightfall to leave."

"I have no intention of leaving. I chall—"

"Before ye say the words, know the laws. When the Alpha is incapacitated, his enforcer fights for him."

Kenna snorts. "Good. Killing Duane will be a bonus."

"Not Duane." Rohan smiles like the evil fucker he is, and there's a provocative glint in his eye.

"You can't mean you," Kenna crows. "You left the clan."

"I left the town, not the clan."

Gloriana wrings her hands, her eyes on me. She's nervous. I smell her fear, and I wish I could comfort her, but sometimes even the strongest of us fall and need time before they can get back up.

During that time, other people fight our battles as we would fight them. It's how loyalty works. It's what being a lycan means. Rohan is prepared to die for me, and I only hope Kenna takes the out he's giving her and leaves.

While she might be able to win a challenge over Rohan, I'm certain Rohan has a plan for my security during the challenge and for my safety in case he loses. I would live one way or the other, and Kenna knows the only way to get rid of me is to kill both me and my mate.

Soft footsteps pad away. Kenna is gone, though how far remains to be seen.

For now, my mate is safe.

27

LENOX

The news that I'll survive the wounds reaches the clan three spans after the tavern incident. In the meadow, my lycans celebrate, and all I can do is lie in bed and wonder if my mate is with them.

She loves gatherings. I want to give her as many gatherings as her heart desires. But supervised because I go crazy thinking about lycan males surrounding her.

Even if our mating bond has solidified, and I sense that she loves me as much as I love her, and she is as committed to me as I am to her, I still cannot stand the thought of other males even speaking with her.

Which is why I hate that my recovery is taking forever and a span. Still bedbound, using most of my energy on regrowing the skin on my belly, I tire quickly and fade in and out of consciousness.

The door opens, and I lift my head slightly.

It's Rohan. He's carrying what looks like leather belts and a hammer. Closing the door behind him, he smiles like an evil sly fox.

He's up to no good.

I clear my throat to ask what's going on, but he presses a claw over his lips. "It's best if you don't whine, Alpha."

Whine? Cocksucker. I will never live down the fact I couldn't speak and that when I tried, it sounded like whining. And since I'm surrounded by a bunch of cocksuckers and comedians, now that I'm on the way to recovery, the clan is making fun of the dramatics that took place during my recovery.

At least something is giving them joy.

Kenna's departure was hard on everyone. Betrayal is hard, especially when the offending party is allowed to recover and possibly strike again later. But enemies have always targeted the clan, and I've always found a way to protect them.

Rohan holds out leather straps and smiles from ear to ear, his icy-blue lycan eyes twinkling with excited magic. "Bought these from the fairies."

What are they? I want to ask, but a low growl that indeed sounds like something between a whine and a wheeze comes out. I watch Rohan nail the leather straps to each of the bedposts.

He grabs my ankle.

I catch on quickly. *No fucking way.* I bend my knees.

He smirks. "You'll tire. Surrender."

Never!

He grabs my other ankle. I jerk my leg back, and the pain in my belly and lungs makes me wish I would pass out again. My chest moves up and down, and Rohan waits.

"You chained me to your bed, Lenox. Marybell found me that way, tried to free me, but couldn't. Guess who she called for help?"

Inwardly, I smile. *Who?*

"Fleur. You know." He grabs my ankle, and I let him because I might die of laughter.

He pulls my foot through the leather strap and tightens it, then reaches for my other ankle and does the same.

"The fairy princess found me chained to your bed." He pulls out a pretty green peacock feather from the pocket of his kilt.

What's that for? I wonder.

"The princess couldn't get the chains off either, so she called the prince."

I laugh.

My lungs might collapse.

But I can't stop.

I'm wheezing and whining, and although it doesn't sound like laughter, I twist my body to the side, tears coming out of my eyes.

"It gets better," he says. "The prince and Fleur and Marybell were all in the chamber working to get your chains off my body and when they couldn't, they called the royal guard. Luckily for me, the commander of the fae armies, a male who did not find it amusing, answered the summons of his prince. He freed me, but not before the entire court heard about it, and the Summer prince wondered how he missed the fact I like playing with my Alpha."

I can't stop laughing.

Something swipes across my soles.

It's the feather.

He moves it over my sole again, and the reflex makes me wiggle my toes.

Next, he dances his claws over the sole of my foot.

Stop it.

He won't stop.

The door opens, and Gloriana enters on quiet feet.

"Oh good. He's awake. I thought he might want a sip of the new horde bourbon that Queen Jo sent me." My mate circles the bed.

She's wearing her hair up, exposing my marking and the curve of her slender neck. Moreover, she's wearing a mended short dark green skirt and a red top with a slit that reaches midbelly, exposing a generous view of her fine tits. She looks fuckable and makes me instantly hard.

My knob rises as my mate rests her knee on the bed and leans over to kiss me on the mouth.

She's been drinking bourbon. She smiles down at me with kindness and love. The expression doesn't last long because her gaze travels down my body to where my erect cock is making a dent in the sheets while my ankles are strapped by the leather belts nailed to the bedposts, with Rohan at the end of the footboard.

He smiles and brushes the feather over my foot again.

My toes curl.

"Tickle, tickle."

28

GLORIANA

Lenox's body heals incredibly fast.

The severe burns and damaged muscle were repaired in less than half a cycle, and now thin transparent skin is covering his upper body. Since he's covered in skin now and almost back to normal, I can touch him again. And so I do.

It's late in the morning, and the weight of his body, held up by his elbows, lies on top of me. We're upside down on the bed, our heads where our feet should be. Lenox moves us this way.

We don't speak.

We make out.

I've missed his touch.

Oh, how I've missed his touch.

I think he missed mine too, because he groans into my mouth and trails a hand down my leg to hook two fingers behind my knee and lift the leg so he can grab my ankle. He moves my leg up and secures it through the leather strap hanging from the bedpost and does the same with my other ankle. I'm spread wide open for him, my legs strapped by the ankles.

A thick finger enters me as we make out, and I grab the sheets instead of his chest hair or the hair on his head while he probes me. At first, he's gentle, but then he adds another finger and starts pumping them.

I claw at the sheets.

Lenox breaks the kiss and whispers in my ear, "This little pussy missed something fat inside her, didn't she?"

"Yes, wolf."

"What's a good little lass say when she wants lycan knob?"

"Please, wolf, let me have your knob."

He spanks me. "That's not what the lass says." He lifts his palm and lands it on my bottom. Several times.

I grit my teeth while my body catches fire with the arousal pulsing inside my channel and pushing out liquid heat for mating the lycan.

"The lass says," Lenox corrects, his facial features gaining harder edges. He spits on his finger and starts pushing it inside my small pucker hole. "The lass says, 'Please, wolf, knob me.'"

"Please, wolf, knob me." My eyes roll to the back of my head at the feel of his finger probing my ass.

"You're relaxed now. Way to go, lass. You're made for me, you trust me, you know I will fuck you nice and hard." He removes his finger from my back hole, and I miss it, though not for long. At my pussy, he presses his large cock and enters me slowly, folding his body over me again and hugging me so that when he fucks me, I do nothing but let go. I let go of everything when Lenox has his way with me.

It's a wonderful feeling.

To be taken care of.

To be under his control.

To surrender.

Lenox loves me and cares for me, and he comes inside me. The knob end swells, and I snap open my eyes as if coming out of a daze.

His knob end is stretching my pussy. He watches me from above, leaning on one hand so he can release my legs with the other hand. His arms flex and so do his chest muscles. I run my palm over his hairless torso. As much as I loved the hair, I also love seeing his muscles flex. He's an incredibly fit male. An Alpha.

And he's mine.

The knob end hooks us together as it swells inside me.

"How does it feel?" he asks, looking worried.

"I'm a little peeved you haven't knotted me until now."

He chuckles, and it's sexy as heck.

"Yer pussy was too narrow for the knob end."

"Bet you liked that."

"I did."

I cup his face. "I'm so happy you're feeling better."

He kisses me. "I love you, little lass."

"I love you too, big wolf."

Lenox snaps his head toward the window and tilts his head as a wolf would when he's listening. To me, it looks as if he's confused, which I find cute if slightly alarming because I can't hear anything.

Not for long.

A commotion outside soon reaches my ears. People are shouting and horses are neighing.

"What is it?" I ask as his knob end releases us.

He tilts his head further, trying to hear better, so I say

nothing more but rise to walk to the window and peer down. It's a convoy of carriages. Kilseleian royal carriages. My carriages.

29

GLORIANA

I shriek and toss on the first dress I grab from the wardrobe before dashing out of the chambers as fast as my legs will carry me, almost knocking over the tray a confused Rohan is carrying.

Every morning before breakfast, and sometimes even after, Rohan visits and brings Lenox food. Once, I found Rohan sleeping on our bed in his wolf form.

It was a particularly difficult span for Lenox, the span when his breathing was so erratic, I thought he might die of heart failure.

Mackenzie said Rohan is a male who Lenox trusts, and so having him nearby guarding me while Lenox couldn't calmed the Alpha wolf and allowed him to use all the energy on self-healing.

Outside, a grand purple-and-black carriage with my father's old seal mounted at the top waits for me. The door opens, and Marybell pokes her head out, gazing up and everywhere at once, her mouth half-agape.

I remember when I first beheld the den of wolves, and realize my expression must've been the same. The sight is that of beautiful wilderness, and for the first time in over a turn, I want to capture the den on canvas.

Marybell's gaze lands on me. She doesn't wait for anyone to bring the stairs so she can step from the carriage gracefully. She hops off and runs. I meet her halfway, and we hug and jump up and down, all the while squealing in joy.

"I missed you so much, milady," she says.

"I missed you more."

"No way. You were shagging the hot lycan while I was packing the trunks and dealing with the dreadful fae royals."

"Since when are the fae royals dreadful?"

"Since the prince kept adding trunks of his clothes to the carriage."

"What?"

She nods, her pretty brown locks slipping out from under the gray cap that keeps her hair tidy while she works. "Prince El'jah sent his stuff. Says you owe him a party and he'll be coming through the portal the lycan never closed." She leans in conspiratorially. "That last part he whispered in my ear."

"Did he, now?"

Marybell blushes. "He did, milady, and I nearly fainted from a desire to have him take me on the marble floor of your former room, so let me tell you, I'm happy to leave the fae court. All that...beauty gets a bit overstimulating for me. I'm happy to be here, where there's not so much temptation."

"Oh, Marybell." I swallow.

"What?"

I point behind her as the carriages start clearing out, leaving an open view of the meadow and the forest beyond. Magic is bursting at the edges of the forest, and nude lycan males are emerging and walking across the meadow.

I glance at Marybell, whose eyes are as big as dinner plates.

"You can see now why Prince El'jah wants me to throw a party in the lycan den."

"I see and can never unsee." She turns to me. "So much for less temptation."

I giggle.

"You are still the person I wanted to see most."

"And I you. Shall we?" I thread my hand under her elbow and pull her inside the den, realizing I've only ever seen our chambers and I can't very well take Marybell there. Where will she stay? Frowning, I walk the long hallway and reach our room, but don't go inside.

"I don't know where your rooms will be," I say.

Marybell frowns at me. "What do you mean?"

"You know how you stay next to me all the time?"

She nods.

"Well, it's not like that here."

"How is it?"

"Um, well, for one, they have no servants."

Marybell blinks. "Do you mean to tell me the lycan Alpha is changing his own chamber pot?"

"The lycan Alpha pisses on trees."

She gasps, then covers her mouth. "You have been changing your own pot?"

My turn to nod.

"My princess, are you saying you do not need me anymore?"

Oh no! "That's not what I'm saying at all. Lots has happened around here, and I... I failed to make arrangements for your arrival."

She smiles. "I am not a lady anymore, and my arrival is not of importance."

"You are a lady and an important one to me."

"Hey," Mackenzie greets us from the other end of the hallway and strides up to us. She jerks her chin at Marybell. "Hey, I'm Mackenzie, the clan princess."

Marybell curtsies and stays low.

Mackenzie curtsies as well. I think she likes the way the Kilseleians greet each other. She also curtsies with so much grace that it's a pleasure to watch the fluid movement of her body.

Mackenzie's eyes dart from me to Marybell. "Why are you two standing at the door like lost pups?"

"Marybell needs a room next to mine."

"There are no rooms next to yours."

"Which is why I'm standing here not knowing where to take her."

"You can stay with me," Mackenzie offers.

Marybell blushes, her gaze darting to me.

I explain. "Marybell's family has served the Kilseleian crown for two centuries. She will stay with me till death do us part. It is inappropriate for her to stay with another princess."

Mackenzie swats the air. "I was kidding about the princess part. I'm not a princess. I'm the Alpha's sister is all."

"Still," I say, "Marybell stays near me." I don't want her to feel like I no longer need her, even if it's true that I don't need her to serve me. I need her friendship.

"The closest place to your chambers is the nursery," Mackenzie says.

I blink. Lenox mentioned a nursery once, but I thought he was speaking of a nursery he plans on furnishing in the distant future.

"Milady, I will settle myself. Please don't burden yourself."

"Show us to the nursery," I say.

Mackenzie nods, and we follow her down the hallway and take a right instead of a left. We hit a wall. Or what I think is a wall, but Mackenzie shoves it with her shoulder, and it creaks, dust flaking off, cobwebs stretching and breaking as Mackenzie walks in.

She sneezes, dust likely tickling her sensitive nose.

It's a steep stairway leading into what looks like the depth of hell.

Mackenzie descends.

We do not.

"Milady?"

"What's wrong?" Mackenzie asks, her blue eyes blazing like beacons in the pitch-dark night.

"We're scared of the dark and we can't see," I say.

"Oh!" She returns and rounds the corner of the main hallway. We wait for her and chat, and I hear Lenox's voice. Expecting him to join us and greet Marybell, I figure we'll see him later, when Mackenzie returns alone with a pair of lanterns.

"We can reach the nursery through secret hallways from the main chambers. My brother has to approve Marybell's access to that passage, so we're going from here until then. Ready now?"

Lanterns in hand, Marybell and I descend the steps, and Mackenzie opens the door. We step into another hallway and through three more doors until we reach a metal door Mackenzie shoves open with her shoulder.

"I feel like we're entering a treasury and there's gonna be gold on the other end," Marybell whispers, probably thinking Mackenzie can't hear her since she's already inside the dark space.

We step into the room and lift the lanterns.

More than a dozen wooden cribs stand on thick colorful elven carpets. The room is painted in every color of the rainbow. Mackenzie releases the light bugs kept in stasis and they light up the space. All I can say is, "They're all empty."

Mackenzie smiles a little bit on the sad side. "I'm the youngest in the clan and technically not even a full-blooded lycan."

"What do you mean?" Marybell asks.

"Territorial clan wars mean the lycan goddess favored male births for centuries. We have a shaky peace now, but the damage has been done. You and my brother are the first mated pair in a long while, and when he recognized what you were to him, he started making the cribs."

"Awww," Marybell says as she runs her palm over a wooden crib rail.

It hits me then. The purpose. The meaning. I have a purpose. It's always been there, though it's just that I see it now. One's purpose is difficult to see when life sucks, when lemons instead of water rain down on your happy parade.

When the savages came, I lost my country and my tiara.

When the lycan claimed me, I hated him for taking away my freedom.

But looking back, all those events led me here, where I'm a mate to an Alpha of a lycan clan and a princess to a group of people that need me to survive in said clan.

"Marybell," I say, squaring my shoulders. "Go to town with Mackenzie and invite every Kilseleian female of childbearing age to the den for a *sparty*."

"What is a sparty, milady?"

"It's a party we will have in the den's spas. A ball in swimsuits."

"Why only females?" Mackenzie asks.

I raise an eyebrow. "You don't have enough males to pick from here?"

"None of them will touch me."

Stunned, I blink. "Why not?"

"Lenox is my brother. Duh."

"Oh no, Lenox is cockblocking you."

She nods. "If I stay in the clan, I will die a virgin."

"What about the mission to have babies?" Marybell asks. "You are a female."

"It doesn't apply to his sister."

I laugh. "I'll talk to Lenox. Marybell, you didn't happen to bring any paintings, did you?"

"All of them."

"You're the best." I turn on my heel and climb up the stairs, knowing exactly where I'm headed. "The bare walls could use some art. I'm going to fetch some paintings. Don't tell Lenox. I want to surprise him."

I hang the lantern on one of the hooks near the wall and proceed outside, where the males have taken care of the horses and only the few carriages from the back of the convoy remain.

Unfortunately, there's no method to the carriage madness, meaning I have no idea which carriage carries the paintings, but I know that they're transported on the roof of one of the square carriages. There are three square carriages.

I walk down the lineup, my gaze turned upward so that only the corner of my eye catches a blurry mass of fur coming at me.

I scream right before I'm flying through the air and hit the back of my head on the wall. The world goes dark.

30

LENOX

A *while before*

Now I can say I've been fried.

Like a potato.

I was fried by a magical blood shield that left me fighting for my life the moment the adrenaline wore off.

After Gloriana leaves to greet her staff, I finally rise from the bed. The mirror reflects a hairless male with smooth transparent skin under which muscles filled with blood and ligaments flow and flex, showing signs of a healthy recovery. I have no idea what's taking so long for my hair to grow back, though. It's closing in on a cycle since I sustained my injuries.

The females outside the chambers are chatting, and I'm listening in on them. They're trying to decide where Marybell will stay. I think she ought to stay with my sister, but she insists on being close to Gloriana, which immediately puts a smile on my face.

I also want to be close to Gloriana.

My princess has two people looking out for her. It's a great thing.

My princess having the entire clan looking out for her is even better.

Which is why I need to get out of my chambers and into the dining hall I hoped my hair would grow back before I had to show my face in front of the clan so that they'd think everything is back to the way it was. Everything will be fine. I'm fine, but the hair is stubbornly not growing back fast enough. They must see me.

And the hair is what it is. It might not grow back at all.

Now I understand why my princess and the fairies keep up their appearances. Perception is part of the power plays people growing up in the courts understand. Having hair somehow makes me whole, and a whole Alpha brings security to the pack.

I grab my new dark gray leather kilt and throw a belt that's green with red fur over it, showing our clan colors. I pull the belt through the clan's banner and let the banner hang over my left hip and down my side.

Ready, I lean my shoulder against the door and continue listening to the females. The moment the topic of the nursery comes up, I press my ear to the door. As if that's necessary. With the way Mackenzie talks, a lycan could hear her down at the docks.

Gloriana doesn't comment on the topic of babies, and I'm disappointed, but not too much so, since the females are heading down to the nursery.

I bet Mackenzie didn't bring lanterns.

Before I exit, I grab a pair and head after them. I see Mackenzie walking back.

"Oh." She stops, wide-eyed, my appearance clearly startling her. I used to have a mane of hair on my head and face and chest, and now I'm a walking red baby's bottom.

Her expression explains why Rohan limited the number of visits while I was sick, and I forbade Mackenzie from coming in at all. In case I died, I wanted my sister to remember me as a strong Alpha, not a weak, fried wolf at the mercy of the goddess.

Her eyes fill with tears, but she's holding in the emotion as I pass her the lanterns and kiss her on top of her pretty and smart and lovely head. "I'm fine, pup."

She wraps her arms around my waist and holds on tight. "I have to go because the Kilseleian females can't see in the dark. They're scared. But I'm so happy to see you're well. If bald." She looks up and winks.

I chuckle. If we can make fun of me, we are healthy. We part ways, and I throw over my shoulder as I head outside, "Make sure the females eat breakfast."

"Yes, Alpha."

The moment I step outside, I turn up my face and close my eyes, allowing myself to feel the sun bathe my face.

I missed nature.

Being confined indoors isn't for me.

I inhale a lungful of horses along with their shite, lycan male scents, the fresh ground after last night's summer shower, and the evergreen forest.

Nice.

Something splatters on my shoulder.

It's bird crap. A tiny white-and-gray mass.

I stare at it, unsure if it's a bad omen or a lucky charm.

I wipe it off, then clean my hand on the kilt and proceed

to the dining hall nodding at several gaping males as they spot me. They're staring as if they've never seen me before, and by the time I walk inside, I'm grinding my teeth. In the lineup for food, I move along as if it's any other span, but they don't. They're still staring.

Agitated, I growl, throw some eggs on my plate, then take a seat at my table to get on with eating.

A male sits across from me.

I expect Rohan, but it's Duane.

And he's bald.

"What the fuck happened to yer hair?"

"You're a fashion icon." He winks.

The males are adjusting. I howl.

The clan responds.

And just like that, the stability in the clan is restored.

Kenna left us, even took some of her loyal lycans with her, and that's fine with me. She no longer belongs in the clan. She couldn't operate under my authority when she had to in order to survive. I can't forgive her and will never forget her treason, and if I catch her on clan grounds again, I'll kill her.

She knows that, and so she will stay away. I'm certain of it. As for a replacement, I have Rohan to settle into a new role. Hmm, I'm unsure what Duane is doing here eating with me, though.

I get right to it. "You've seen yer father, I presume."

Duane grunts.

"Has he visited with yer mother yet?"

"No, and if he comes near her, I'll—"

"You will do nothing, Duane."

The boy growls, "Dammit, Alpha, that's none of your business."

"Peace in the clan *is* my business, and you and yer father need to make amends with each other."

"Never."

I wipe my mouth. "Mend yer fucking ways. That's an order, lad."

He stands with me, and we're chest to chest. Yeah, he's growing into his dominance. I smell it. It's irritating. I need to find him something to do besides pick fights with me or his dad.

He grits his teeth, but I sense something terrible coming and react immediately because I trust my instincts. I press a hand over his mouth and shout, "Silence!"

The cantina turns into a graveyard, so quiet that when a female lycan snarls and my princess yelps, magic explodes in the room.

I burst into my werewolf form and sprint outside faster than if taken by fairy portal, the clan following behind me. Across the meadow and around the corner, I arrive to see my princess lying unmoving, blood pooling around her head, Kenna hovering over her.

Not caring that Kenna is an Alpha female needed for the survival of the lycan people, not caring that she's a lifelong friend, not caring whether I'm coming from the back or the front, I lunge.

Before she has time to turn, I close my jaws around her neck, digging my canines deep inside. I twist and hold until Kenna hits the ground, unmoving under me.

Quickly wiping my mouth, I check on my princess. She's alive, but breathing shallowly. "Oh no. No no no. No, my lass. Not my lass." I pull her against my chest and realize I have no healers in the clan.

I have no healers.

I lean back against the wall and rock her as if that will help. I hear her heart slowing, and I know she's leaving me.

She is leaving me.

There is nothing I can do.

The wolves, on all fours, surround me, brushing their fur against me, trying to comfort me as I bring my lass closer so that her face lies on my shoulder and I can hear her tiny breaths for a little while longer.

My thumb touches my marking on the back of her neck. I rub the dents my teeth left only a little while ago. I know this comforts her.

Closing my eyes, I pray. "If you spare her life and keep her with me, I will owe you. In this life or the next, I will owe you. Ask of me anything."

I keep thumbing the marking, praying against hope, when my thumb starts tingling, my hand glowing a faint yellow.

Elven yellow.

The magic my mother possessed.

It seems to accumulate on my thumb, so I rub the marking harder, and soon, Gloriana's heartbeats pick up pace, and she starts breathing more steadily.

Next thing I know, her eyes flutter open and she sits up, but then holds her head. I open my mouth to say something, but bird poo splatters on my chest. Both an omen and a lucky charm.

Some of the wolves shift back into males. I look up, finding Duane.

"Secure the perimeter," I say.

"What should we do if we find traitors on the run?"

"Let them run. Sweep again at dawn. If any are caught on the clan lands, we won't show mercy."

Groaning, Gloriana tries to get up, but I can't let go. If I press her any closer, I might squeeze her too hard. I want her to live inside me so that I can protect her and nothing can touch her.

Having taken on my healing magic, her hazel eyes glow. She looks immortal. My forever lass.

Her gaze drifts to Kenna, then she looks away. "I'm sorry."

"I'm not." A threat to my mate had to be dealt with. I tried to avoid killing Kenna and I would have let her live out her life elsewhere, but she came after my mate and I did what I had to do.

"I want to show you something," Gloriana says.

Fine. Fine. I can let her go. Standing, I shake out my shoulders as the clan mates clear away Kenna's body. Gloriana opens the door to one of the carriages, then, instead of sitting inside, she climbs up the damn thing. Oh, hell, no.

"Get down from there," I say just as she bends over the roof, her short dress riding her thighs, her pussy peeking from between her legs. I lick my lips, my brain hazy with lust for a moment.

Gloriana looks back and speaks. I shake my head. "What?"

"Can you get this painting down for me?"

Mmhm. I can do that.

I grab her hips and help her down, then reach for the third painting in the stack, the one Gloriana ripped at the corner, probably to identify it.

I hand it to her, and she walks over to the wall and leans the painting against it before tearing the gray wrapping paper off.

It's a picture of nature. The sun rises above a forest at the bottom of which a wolf with obsidian fur sits, his posture relaxed, his nose turned down, blue eyes blazing.

It takes me several moments of staring to identify the forest as the same one where I met my princess, and it takes me even longer to realize the wolf looks like me. It's me. She had said she painted me.

The way she sees me in wolf is not the way I imagined I appeared. She painted me with silky, not coarse, long dark hair, and there's a glow about me that's...eternal.

"When did you...? What...?" I'm at a loss for words. Since I recognized Gloriana as my mate, I've spent turns convinced the mating was one-sided. That a Kilseleian female couldn't possibly feel the mating bond at inception and return the mark. But I was wrong.

I was so wrong.

"You saw me as yours," I say. "That morning on yer estate, you saw me."

She shakes her head. "I didn't see you, Lenox. I felt your presence. I felt you, and my brain conjured up this image and wouldn't let it go until I painted it. After I painted it, I hung it above my bed at home and at the estate. It made me feel safe." She walks up to me and rises on her toes. I dip my head so she can kiss me and say, "I love you. Thank you for being there for me, now and forever more."

EPILOGUE

G loriana
A little while later...

THE *SPARTY* IS HAPPENING.

The moment Lenox caught on that his wolves were showing up to the sparty groomed and looking as handsome as ever so that my Kilseleian ladies-in-waiting would mingle with them and flirt, he declared the sparty a hit and pronounced it a lunar event.

Or perhaps he wanted to hold it every new moon because he saw how this party pleased me.

How social events make me happy.

And that I'm a lover of people.

Lenox said I must host as many parties as I please—within the den grounds, because that's where he can best protect me.

The lights are dim, the conversations loud, and the music invites flirtation. With Prince El'jah in attendance and the news of the entire clan being invited to the Summer Court for the royal wedding, that's all everyone is talking about.

Everyone apart from Rohan, who is standing alone, looking awkward during a party where most people are barely dressed. As far as I know, he's single, and more than five of my ladies have asked about him. The lycan is tall, with dark hair and piercing blue eyes. Very handsome and pleasantly playful.

The personality change has me worried.

Since the Summer Court is in mating season and El'jah brought a fae group, their scents mixed with the lycans' horny ones and make my nipples perk as I pad, barefoot, over to Rohan.

"I didn't take you for a brooding type."

A corner of his mouth lifts. "I'm not."

"You are now."

He shrugs. "Have a lot on my mind."

"Is there something I can help with?"

He shakes his head.

"Is there something Lenox can help with?"

Rohan chuckles. "Are you offering for him?"

"Maybe."

"That a lass." He winks, then tips his head, gaze still focused across the vast underground space. I follow the direction of his focus, and Lenox's blue eyes meet mine.

I wave at my mate.

He looks like he's gonna go furry on Rohan.

"I wonder how long he'll last before he marches over here," Rohan says, then brings his cheek to mine. Affectionately, he pecks my temple and sniffs, lingering. I hear him inhaling loudly. "Your scent is lovely."

"Thank you. I no longer wear perfume, so that's nice to hear."

"You have no idea, do you?"

I frown. "About what?"

Rohan smirks and looks at Lenox, who's walking toward us. "Bring us the bubbly drink while you're at it," Rohan says in a normal tone, but Lenox has super hearing. He swipes a bottle from the tray and then shooter glasses from the corner stand.

Lenox strides over to us. "Rohan." My mate wears a short black leather kilt over his middle, showcasing his entire body. He's carved out of a mountain, his muscles a perfect collection of peaks and valleys that I trace with my tongue whenever I please.

He also wears an annoyed expression as he pours us drinks and passes the glasses around.

"The bubbly is served in flutes," Rohan says. "Ye brute."

I chuckle as I see Lenox smile.

Rohan holds up his shooter. "To beginnings."

Three glasses clink together before we drink the liquor.

"Another toast," Lenox says and pours again. "To the trade deal."

"Ah yes, the trade deal," Rohan says less enthusiastically than I'd have expected. The Summer Court struck a textile trade deal with Clan McMar. Since the Summer Court is preparing for the royal wedding, they need more merchandise than ever before, and while some of the ships are en route, the others are waiting on their pirate captain.

"How are the trip preparations going?" I ask.

Rohan scrubs his jaw. "Slow," he says, thoughtfully. In fact, Rohan is mysteriously distracted tonight. While I understand not everyone likes to mingle with people, standing alone during social events seems out of character for this male.

"Are you well?" I ask him.

He nods, and I glance at Lenox, who knows something I don't.

"Maybe he needs another drink," Lenox says. He offers the third round. I extend a hand to accept the shooter, but Rohan covers the glass.

When both Lenox and I stare at him, he lifts an eyebrow. "What? Don't tell me, Alpha. You don't know either."

"Know what?"

Rohan chuckles evilly. "Your princess is pregnant."

I gasp.

Lenox sucks in a breath.

Rohan licks his lips. "And now that I've delivered the news of the little peas in your belly, we can start further securing the den, and I can move on with my life."

Lenox says nothing, even though I have a feeling Rohan is trying to make conversation.

"What will you do?" I ask.

He scrubs his beard and curses. "She hates me."

"Who?" I ask.

"Duane's mother." He tries to take the bottle from Lenox, but he's not giving it up.

"But you love her?" I pry.

"That's right."

"I'm sure you two can work it out. Again." I have no idea what I'm talking about, but I want to support him.

"You think so?" he asks as if hanging on every word.

"Everyone deserves another chance."

"Even arseholes like me?"

"Especially the arseholes." After all, Lenox tackled and

bit me, then practically kidnapped me from the Summer Court and brought me here.

"Alpha, I'll want to speak with you after you're done freaking out," Rohan says, then leaves us.

"Hey." I touch Lenox's hairless chest. His hair hasn't grown back yet. "Are you okay?"

Blinking as if in a trance, he looks down at me and lowers his head to sniff. "So that's what that is."

"Can you smell our babies?"

He nods, a smile spreading over his face. He picks me up and lands a kiss on me that has the clan hooting. "I didn't think I could love you any more than I did a moment ago, but I do." His blue eyes brighten with excitement. "We're pregnant."

"We are."

Lenox walks toward the exit.

"Where are you taking me?"

"Our room."

I laugh. So much for the sparty.

***

Hi, Milana here. Thank for reading! I'm so happy the lycan finally got his happy ending with the Princess. As we move through the Lycan Claimed series, this couple keeps showing up so if you enjoyed them rest assured we will hang out with them some more.

If this is your first ride in my fantasy world, you are in for a treat because this story is a part of a bigger world with fae and savage horde you can reference toward the end of the book. Don't worry, I have links to books you can check at the back but before that, sneak a peak into Rohan's story coming up next...

SECOND CHANCE FOR THE LYCAN TEASER

It's always been the three of us.

My twin, Freya, and me.

And since we both loved her and she loved us back, she was ours, and Roger and I agreed neither will marry her.

I honored my end of the deal. He didn't.

When I came back from a long trip on the seas, I found them as a married couple with her belly swollen with a child.

Naturally, I challenged my twin.

Freya got in the middle of the fight, and I almost ended her life.

To save her from the mess the three of us made, and to avoid murdering my brother, I returned to the seas.

Now I'm back, and I want what he once took from me. My brother's passing means I finally get a second chance with a female who should've always been mine.

Problem is she hates me and has refused to see me ever since I told my son Duane I'm his father, something she and my brother Roger failed to mention. Whether Freya likes me or not, the clan Alpha has ordered a lockdown, and given me an excuse to face her.

During lockdown, all members of the clan must come into the den where the clan patrol heavily protects the grounds. Apparently, everyone except Freya.

I'm not surprised.

The rules never applied to her anyway.

She's one of only three known omega female wolves born among all the clans in the last century, and the only omega in my clan. Lenox, our alpha, makes exceptions for her.

Who wouldn't? Freya is omega cuteness overload.

Petite, red-haired, freckled, and a fireball, she would make these tiny fists and punch me in the belly whenever she'd get mad. That was when we were kids. She'd knee me in the sac later as we grew older.

She liked arguing.

With me.

Not so much with Roger.

In the forest, at the tree trunk where Freya carved Roger's name, marking his burial site, I drop wildflowers near the base before squaring my shoulders and straightening my belt. As I step out of the cover of the trees, Freya opens the front door of my old home.

Inwardly cursing, I slide behind the trunk, secretly watching her as I've done every time I've visited the clan in the past twenty-some turns.

Freya's black skirt sweeps the grass as she makes her way toward the hen house in the back. I hear her talking to the animals, her gentle voice soothing and stroking more than just my knob. It strokes memories, those I drown in liquor while I'm sailing the seas.

When I left, I was certain I could forget her.

Forget how she smiled, laughed, begged while kneeling at the entrance to her nest.

Too bad I couldn't have her before.

But I damn well can have her now.

So when Freya makes her way back toward the house, I step out from the tree and walk toward her. Her long red braided hair bounces off her shoulder as she carries several buckets of water. At the water pump, she tries to fill the buckets, but the pump handle won't budge.

Freya curses.

From right behind her, I falter in my step, not wanting to frighten her, thinking maybe I should walk away and return in the morning.

Or perhaps I shouldn't return at all.

Or perhaps Freya couldn't give three shites about me, and I'm overthinking our reunion.

The last few times I visited the den, she didn't come to meet me, even though Lenox called for a gathering. I've crept up here in the bushes and sat in trees like some sort of stalker just so I could catch a glimpse of her.

The pump seems rusted, not maintained, much like the house and majority of the farm. Choosing to live in seclusion, Freya tends to the old farm alone, which means some things are left neglected.

"Duane," she calls out, likely smelling me and thinking it's our son. "I told you I'm not going in for Lenox's lockdown. Now come here and help me with this pump." She's pressing it down with both hands when I approach from behind and lay my hand over both of hers.

As I bend over her, my nose almost touches the top of her hair, and I inhale the scent of the female I've longed for for decades, one my twin and I couldn't share. One he and I wanted all to ourselves.

"Thanks," she says as the lever is pressed down and water pours.

I can tell the moment Freya realizes I'm not Duane because her body stills, and her heart starts beating loudly, the drumming frantic in my ears.

Reluctantly, I release her soft hands and step back, allowing her time to adjust should she need it.

She does. The sound of her beating heart tells me so.

Freya doesn't turn as I expected. Not right away, anyway.

She fixes her skirt and flips her braid onto her back.

"What are you doing here?" she asks in a trembling voice.

"I've come to collect you for the lockdown."

This isn't how I imagined our reunion would go. To be fair, I didn't know what to expect, because I don't know if there's anything left of what we used to have. It's been over two decades. I'm making a fool of myself.

She picked my brother.

Inviting me into her nest that one time during her heat was a mistake she's probably regretting every time she sees our son. That's not to say she's regretting having him. I'm sure she's proud of him. What's there not to be proud of? Duane has grown into a fine male. An alpha next in line to lead the clan.

Freya clears her throat. "I told Duane I'm staying."

My son has already been here trying to get his mother to come in. Like I said, what's there not to be proud of? "I see."

"Lenox sent you?"

"I came on my own."

"Then you ought to leave."

"I can't."

"Why not? You're great at leaving."

She's bitter. Maybe hurt? If she's hurt, then I have a

chance. Only people we care about can hurt us. "I'm not going anywhere."

Freya snorts. "That line still works with females?"

I grit my teeth. She's bring up my playboy past. Fine. We can do this right away and get it over with. "At least I never married another."

She spins and glares up at me. Tears spill from the corners of her eyes, but Freya wipes them quickly, then picks up the bucket of water, lifts it over her shoulder, and pitches it at me with a battle cry.

Soaking wet, I wipe my face as she stomps into the house and slams the door.

That went well.

ORDER YOUR COPY HERE

ALSO BY MILANA JACKS

Check my website for latest updates and connect with me via email **HERE!**

MORE BOOKS IN THIS FANTASY WORLD

Read the Complete Savage Horde: Savage in the Touch, #1 : Heart, #2 : Need, #3

The Royal Obsession (Summer King)

Lycan Claimed Series:

1. Lycan and the Princess 2. Second Chance for the Lycan (Rohan)

SCI-FI AND FANTASY COMPLETED SERIES

Read the Complete Horde Series:

#1 Alpha Breeds, #2 Alpha Bonds, #3 Alpha Knots, #4 Alpha Collects

The Complete Hordesmen Series:

Hunger #1, Terror #2, Sidone #3, Fever #4, Dreikx #5, The Blind Hordesman #6

Read the complete Tribes Series:

Marked #1, Stolen #2, Lured #3, Captured #4, Consumed #5, Arked #6

Read the complete Beast Mates Series:

#0 Virgin - FREEBIE, #1 Blind, #2 Wild,

#2.5 Goddess, FREE via my Mailing List,

#3 Sent, #3.5 Their, #4 Caught, #5 His, #6 Free.

Read the complete Dragon Brotherhood:

Rise #1, Burn #2, Storm #3, Fight, #4

Short stories in IADB World: Jake 1.5, Eddy #2.5

Read the complete Age of Angels series:

Court of Command, #1 • Court of Sunder, #2 • Court of Virtue, #3

ABOUT THE AUTHOR

Milana Jacks grew up with tales of water fairies that seduced men, vampires that seduced women, and Babaroga who'd come to take her away if she didn't eat her bean soup. She writes sizzling fantasy romance with take charge heroes from her home on Earth she shares with Mate and their three little beasts.

• She entertains readers on her mailing list as they await for books in the series. Join other readers at http://www.milanajacks.com/newsletter/ •

Meet me at
www.milanajacks.com

Printed in Dunstable, United Kingdom